THE BURN

Annie Oldham

The Burn
ISBN-13: 978-1466342064
ISBN-10: 1466342064

For Maggie — my own Jessa — thank you for everything

ONE

The world as we knew it ended in a bang. That was a hundred years ago when the first rumblings of World War III started up, and a rumble was all it took. All the countries that said they never had or had already powered down their nuclear weapons let loose in one fell swoop and *boom!* There goes the neighborhood.

Luckily, I guess, I am a marine biologist's great-granddaughter. After the crisis in Iraq was winding down and things looked like they might actually be relatively peaceful for a while, a group of scientists from all over the world got together—biologists, horticulturists, mechanical engineers, civil engineers, doctors, you name it—and started coming up with a plan. The basic gist was this: if anything like a global catastrophe were to occur, is there anywhere safe on Earth? And all they came up with was the ocean floor.

So they started building. They got funding with grants detailing studies into the life cycles of the weird creatures that

1

deep, how the oceanic plates moved, and finding alternative energy sources. No one flat-out said they were looking to colonize, and nobody asked. They were selfish about it (not all of them, but those who were more altruistic were quickly shushed), being careful who they told and what investors and builders they used, because the last thing they wanted it to look like was a replay of the Titanic—they were obviously first-class passengers and everyone else on the planet was steerage.

They built their first colony in the Pacific Ocean next to the Mariana Trench. Five hundred people went to live there— mostly the scientists and their families, including my great-grandfather (the marine biologist) and my grandmother, who was twenty at the time. They just fed their friends and family some bogus moving story and gave them phony addresses.

Then five years after that, another colony was built in the Atlantic Ocean next to the Puerto Rico Trench. And soon every couple years another colony or two would pop up somewhere else. By the time of the Event (when all the bombs went off), there were fourteen colonies scattered throughout the earth's oceans.

I was born sixteen years ago to a marine biologist dad and a nutritionist mom. Everyone is an -ist down here. I think it makes them feel that they deserve to be down here instead of up there. My dad also happens to be the speaker for the Mariana Colony. My grandma was before him, and now my dad is. It's like being governor. Sure it sounds important, but when you live down here, everyone sounds important. There are just a lot of jobs to do.

I hate it.

Especially on days like today when I don't have school, I don't have my scheduled "introspection" time, I don't have my field studies. I don't have *anything* to keep my mind occupied. I just have my job. Everyone gets a job when they're twelve—selected "with all your aptitudes and interests in mind"—and most of them stick with it. I'm on my fifth job since then—I changed every year. Well, I guess I should admit I changed twice in one year, too.

I've tried structural design, but I fell asleep about five times before they decided to switch me. I tried medicine, but no one liked my bedside manner. After old Earl Kather finally marched to my dad's office with his gown hanging open in the back and complained, they *finally* gave me another job. I tried culinary arts, but after I burned some hot chocolate, the sous chef rolled his eyes and shooed me away for the last time. I've tried marine biology like my dad, but I hate going down the Trench. There are beacon lights every fifty feet for the first quarter mile, and after that it's nothing but blackness. There's too much of that living down here. I didn't want any more.

My current vocation is agriculture. Yes, dress me up in overalls and give me a straw hat. Well, not quite. (Though that's not how it was when the bombs went off—or so Rint Klein, my history teacher, tells me.) I wear a solar radiation suit. The lights we have over our artificial fields simulate real sunlight, so if I were in there for too long, I'd get a sunburn just like if I was on a beach. I guess up on the Burn (that's what we call the land) they had something called sunscreen, but then some dermatologist down here designed the solar radiation suits and said they were much more effective protection. Sometimes I want to smack him.

Today is my work day, and I go to the pod that opens onto Field #3. The fields are huge domes that sit half in the colony and half under the crushing ocean. If you were to look down on us from above, you'd see five fields all bubbling out on the west side of the colony. The field is covered in a big dome of UVA/UVB filtering borosilicate, so you can peek in at what's growing, but the solar radiation can't escape and toast everyone walking by. There are temperature regulators, solar lamps, and air regulators all hanging from the top of the dome. You go through the door of the pod, and then there's a door on the opposite side that leads to the field. The pod is a small room about ten feet square with lockers on one side for the workers for this field, a bench down the middle of the room, and showers on the opposite side.

I run a hand through my short, black hair and stuff the helmet on my head. I talk my claustrophobia into submission. My therapist (which we are all required to see at least monthly) said the claustrophobia would ease up as I got used to the suit. I'm thinking I might be in for another vocation. That'll be three in one year. I will never live it down.

My sister, Jessa, and my friend Brant walk in through the sliding door, grab their suits from their lockers, and suit up. Jessa looks just like me—black hair (but hers is long—luxurious, some girls call it), green eyes, short but strong—but where my skin is fair bordering on translucent, hers is coppery. She got that from my mom.

Jessa is my only sibling. I should have four more sisters, but things happened. There's a law down here—each couple can only have two kids. Something about sustainable populations and all that. But when my mom and dad got pregnant and went

4

to their first pre-natal appointment, the doctor told them they were having sextuplets. My mom was so happy she started crying. She'd always wanted a big family, and knew it wasn't possible. Maybe this was how it needed to happen. But my dad, Mr. Speaker of the Mariana Colony, just worried about what it would do to his reputation—the speaker who broke laws.

He pulled the doctor aside and asked what could be done. The doctor just stared at him. When my dad explained his concern, the doctor said that surely this would be an acceptable breach of protocol. A couple in another colony five years ago had triplets, and that was allowed. People treated it almost like a fulfillment of prophecy or something. My dad asked if aborting four of the fetuses was possible. The doctor said no one in his right mind would condescend to that kind of murder. So he talked my dad down. When my mom went into labor six months later, four of the babies were stillborn, and my sister and I were the only ones who made it. My dad held us like a miracle—like we had something to do with upholding the laws— and he fawned over my mother who gave us to him. To hear my grandma tell it, he was a doting husband and loving father, and my mother couldn't ask for anything more. But then my mom found out about what happened with the doctor. With four of my sisters being stillborn and only two surviving, my mom grew depressed and then suspicious. She moved out of our quarters. When that wasn't far enough, she left the colony. Said she was going to the Puerto Rico Trench colony, half way around the world. But my dad never heard from her again. No one really knows where she ended up.

It tore my dad up, and he threw himself into his work. My grandma moved in to help out. And now I have to live with two speakers of the colony. Sure one's retired, but it feels like they're both on active duty.

My dad never told me this dark chapter of his past. I know about it through the colony's archives. Everything down here is recorded and kept for posterity, if you know how to access it. You really can't have a moment's peace.

"Terra, what's wrong?" Jessa asks. She shakes me right out of that reverie. I flip down my visor and it clicks into place. She carefully ties her long hair into a knot and puts on her helmet. Jessa knows me so well. She can't even see my face through the visor, and she already knows something is bugging me.

"Nothing." My voice crackles through the microphone and into her ear piece under her helmet. "Just wanting to get this over with. Again."

"Liar. And if you actually tried to like it, it might not be that bad, you know." She reaches out a gloved hand and almost touches me.

I can just imagine her motherly look under that helmet, the look she's given me her whole life. But strangely, I don't mind it. Most other people try to be protective (my Dad's a pro at being protective), and I shut off. Not with Jessa. I don't feel like she is condescending. I just feel like she cares.

"I don't care if you like it or not," Brant says, grabbing an aerator. "Let's just get this done fast so we can hit the Juice Deck if we have time."

Jessa raises her visor and kisses him. She grabs a pair of pruners and a bucket and turns to me. Her eyes are bright after the kiss. She snaps her visor back in place.

"You up for irrigation monitoring today?"

I sigh. "Again?"

6

"It beats fertilizer testing."

That is true. All the colony's fields are fertilized with pelagic sediment. At least that's what the marine biologists call it. We call it "the ooze." Or "the crud." Or the "gross stuff on the ocean floor." The ocean floor at this depth has this layer of shells, animal skeletons, and decaying plants and stuff. It's yellowish, and well, oozy. There are people whose job it is to go out and actually harvest the stuff. Blech. At least that hasn't been one of my many vocations.

When it's my day to do fertilizer testing, I just stand around vats of the stuff with big rubber gloves up to my shoulders and poke around in it and take samples to test to make sure it'll help our veggies be good for us. Then I usually start thinking about how eating one our tomatoes is just like slurping a big glass of the ooze. Gross. Best not to think of it. Better yet, best not to even be on the fertilizer testing schedule. I might need a vocation change sooner than I thought.

But I suck it up and go into Field #3 with Jessa and Brant. The field is full of corn. Brant walks around with the aerator, poking holes in the soil around each plant, being meticulous not to damage roots. Brant definitely has what it takes to be a good agriculturist, and I admire him for it. He knows what he wants and goes for it. He never founders.

Jessa takes her pruners and cuts off any dead or sad-looking plant parts and puts them in the bucket. They'll go to fertilizer processing to be added to the composter. Jessa is pretty good at farming, too. Not like Brant—he definitely has the touch. Her speciality is fertilizers and stuff like that, how to feed the plants to make them the most nutritionally dense. Jessa actually *likes*

7

being on fertilizer testing. She has my mom's knack for nutrition.

I make sure that all the plants are equally watered and then adjust the irrigation system controls. Even though I could give her a hard time about it, I appreciate Jessa giving me this job. It requires the least amount of finesse.

As I examine the soil around a plant with browning leaves, Jessa sidles up next to me, absently trimming at the same plant with her pruners.

"For real, Terra, what was bugging you back there?"

I sigh. The temperature control in my suit whirs to life as the thermometer reaches 75 degrees. Except during exercises, I don't think I have ever sweat a day in my whole life. Everything around here is micromanaged.

"Do you ever feel trapped down here? Like there's nowhere to go except where everyone else wants you to?"

"It hasn't gotten any better, has it?"

"No."

Jessa doesn't answer my question because we both know she doesn't understand. We've had this discussion before, and she does try to see where I'm coming from. But she's happy down here, so she just can't get it. She doesn't try to offer advice—she knows there isn't anything she can say that will help—so she just listens better than anyone else can, and tries her hardest to cheer me up. Sometimes it works, but more often than not she leaves frustrated that she can't do more.

She gives me an awkward hug through the radiation suits and bumps her helmet against mine in one of those ridiculous gestures of camaraderie that looks inane, but I know the depth of feeling behind it. I don't want her worrying about me.

8

"I'll be fine."

"We'll have time for the Juice Deck. It'll be fun."

I try to smile.

It takes us four hours to finish up, and then we head out to the Juice Deck. The Juice Deck is on one of the higher levels of the colony and has a huge observation window overlooking the Mariana Trench. A kind of romantic idea, I guess, but at this depth, light doesn't make its way down here, and you can't see anything. There's nothing to see, but for some reason people still want a seat by the window. If you're here in the morning or the evening, you can see the sub going for the trench or coming back, its lights glowing until it disappears in the murk. I don't know why there are windows in this place at all. There's nothing but black and cold all around us. It feels oppressive, and I sit with my back to it, which isn't much better. I feel like something is always watching me.

Brant orders for us: a mango mash for Jessa, a blueberry blast for me, and chocolate chug for him. The Juice Deck serves smoothies and light snacks—all nutritionally optimized, of course.

Brant takes a long swig. "Ow, brain freeze!" He holds his forehead for a moment. "Mmm, that tastes so good after working in the field. How's yours, Jessa?"

Jessa nods, still slurping at hers, closing her eyes in satisfaction. Brant wraps his arm around her shoulders and buries his head in her hair.

"Mmm . . . your hair always smells good. Like strawberries."

Jessa flips her hair over her shoulder. Half the guys our age are in love with her for her hair. A few publicly fantasize about running their fingers through it. It is a shiny, black waterfall. Brant knows he's lucky to be the one to touch it.

I avert my eyes and sip my drink.

"You know, in Mr. Klein's class, he told us that up on the Burn they had something called refined sugar. They added it to smoothies like this, and it made them taste ten times better."

Brant rolls his eyes. "I guess that's something they teach you when you're three grades ahead of everyone else in history. Why don't we have it?"

I shrug my shoulders. "Empty calories."

"Figures," Jessa says.

"Stuff up there was so weird," Brant says. He grabs my smoothie and slurps it.

"Hey!" I swat his arm. He slides my drink back.

Brant and I have been friends for a few years. I ran into him on one of my ill-fated house calls, and now it's like we've known each other since diapers.

Then he met Jessa two months ago, and it was spontaneous combustion. I give credit to Jessa for not letting things get awkward when the three of us are together. He's googly for her, but she keeps it cool when I'm around.

Brant tries a sip of Jessa's smoothie.

"So weird," says Jessa. "I mean, can you believe the mythologies? Those ancient cultures on the Burn believed such crazy stuff. And the most enlightened cultures, too."

Brant grins, leaning close like a conspirator. "Crazy names too, like Zeus, and Hera, and what was the goddess of earth's name? Ga-, Guy-, shoot I can't remember."

"But can you imagine?" I say, not wanting to let the sugar die. "Something tasting better than this?"

10

"Just let it go." Jessa reaches out her hand and touches my elbow. "You talk too much sometimes, and you know it."

I shrug. So what? But I smirk at Jessa—she knows exactly how right she is. She raises an eyebrow at my cheekiness.

"You know what happened the last time you went on about something up on the Burn."

I do remember, and I resent our dad for it. When each kid turns fifteen, they enroll in Mr. Klein's Burn History class as part of the school curriculum. By school board mandate, the first thing they see is old news footage of the Event and its aftermath. It's just in high definition instead of 3D projection, so naturally there's always a few elbow jabs and eye rolls at the primitive technology. But everyone sobers up pretty quickly. Naturally, no one is too curious about the Burn after seeing that carnage.

But after I had been in Mr. Klein's history class for two months, he came to my dad and recommended I be put in a more advanced course. What he didn't tell my dad was why I was so much more advanced. It wasn't my superior intellect (which I don't have), it was just my obsessive fascination with the Burn and anything related to it.

At the time I didn't realize that could be a dangerous thing. After all, we take a history class about the Burn. If they want to teach us about it, how bad can it be? The first day in the advanced course, Mr. Klein taught about scuba divers and submarines, and how primitive ones were crushed by sea pressure. After the Event, some of the survivors salvaged a few remaining submarines and tried to locate the colonies.

So I ran home after school and talked my dad's ear off about scuba divers and submarines. But when I asked him if any of us had gone up there to explore, he just about lost it.

"No one has ever gone up there. No one ever will."

And I had the guts to ask why.

"Nuclear fallout. Roving gangs. Complete anarchy. No reliable plumbing. Take your pick!" His face had gone beyond red and was almost white with anger. "I am never to hear about exploring the Burn, visiting the Burn, or anything related to it unless it is a purely historical, intellectual exercise. Do I make myself clear?"

I had fled to our room. Before I had even closed the door, I heard him sink into the sofa and begin to sob.

"Oh, my love, what can I do better?" Dad always talked to the ghost of my mom when he was in trouble.

Jessa was in our room, studying. I spent the rest of the night curled up against her shoulder, crying.

By morning I had catalogued the excuses: nuclear fallout, gangs, anarchy, plumbing. I would go to Mr. Klein's office and ask about those. It was scheduled introspection, so I knew he'd be in his office instead of teaching.

His office was a small room just off a corridor. One wall was a window covered in bookshelves. You could just catch a few glimpses of the dark ocean between books. He deliberately covered up the dark space. He didn't like a window into night anymore than I did. In a corner was Mr. Klein's desk, all titanium with a couple slots for papers. He hunched over a small laptop, probably working on lesson plans. He ran his fingers through his salt and pepper hair. He wore brown pants and a tweed jacket. No one else wore tweed. But he always said it was the traditional uniform of academics, so he had the colony outfitter produce enough tweed jackets for his lifetime and then tell

12

them they could stop production if they wanted to. The door was ajar, so I rapped on the door frame.

He jumped up and closed his computer in one motion, like he was caught red-handed doing something bad. Weird. Then he turned, squinted, and smiled. A little relieved, I thought, when he saw it was me.

"Hello, Terra, come on in." He gestured to an empty seat by the desk. I sat down quickly, staring at my shoes. I had no idea how to begin this conversation. If being obsessed with the Burn was such a bad thing around here, how did I bring it up with a teacher who could just report back to my dad?

Mr. Klein studied me for a moment. Then he nodded, folded his fingers, and put his hands on his lap.

"You got in trouble with your father?" he said.

I glanced up. "Yeah, how did you know?"

"You'll find that not everyone has an appreciation for the Burn like you or I do."

"But why? It's where we came from. We should know about it. And there's survivors up there! My dad said so. Shouldn't we help them?"

Mr. Klein gave a sad, low chuckle. "You should be easier on your father. He's never been quite the same since your mother left."

"Then maybe he shouldn't have been so stupid!"

Mr. Klein ran a finger around the rim of a mug, ignoring my outburst.

"Did you know in my early teaching days I advocated a new vocation? Burn Exploration. It was shot down before it could even be introduced at committee. And I was strictly warned that if I ever brought up something like that again, I would lose my teaching position. I couldn't be a liability—infecting children's minds with such bad ideas."

He smiled at me, but his eyes were tired and old.

"I had no idea," I whispered. What else could I say?

He nodded. "There are two schools of thought in the colonies. There are the Old. They want to keep life down here a secret. Of course people up there suspect about us. How could they not? But they've never seen any proof, as far as I know. So the Old want to keep it that way. No contact, no exploration. They're afraid there'd be a run on our colonies—people trying to find a better life.

"Then there are people like you and me, Terra. New. People who don't believe the lies about radiation poisoning—and they are lies. Sure a week, two weeks after the Event, conditions were still incredibly dangerous. But after a hundred days, fallout dangers are all but gone. Land can be cleansed and improved. It's been a hundred years. We could all go back up there and resume a normal life. It's true that socially things have been rocky. Understandably so. But they're trying to get their lives together, establish order. Some are succeeding, some aren't."

"How do you know all this? I thought contact with the Burn was illegal."

Mr. Klein's eyes flashed once, as if I'd asked something too close to the mark, and then ignored the question, uncrossing and recrossing his legs as he leaned closer to me. He moved his hands gracefully with his words, as if we were discussing nothing more than this morning's breakfast.

"The trouble is—besides the fact that the Old have more influence—is that the Old can't see past the ends of their noses. They think they've created Eden down here. That they're safe in their high-tech cocoon. But I'm a history teacher, and I know better. You know my mantra in class about history and ignorance?"

"They're doomed to repeat it," I said, seeing where this was going. The Old refused to listen to the past or learn the lessons from it by embracing the Burn. In another hundred years, who knew. Maybe all the colonies would blow themselves to hell and only a few scientists would escape and want to colonize the Burn.

Mr. Klein nodded. "I'm glad you pay attention."

He reached for his coffee and brought it to his lips. Then he paused before taking a sip.

"Up on the Burn, their coffee has caffeine in it. Produces quite a satisfying little buzz of energy." He studied his mug for a moment before continuing.

"I know how you feel about life down here, Terra. We've had a lot of conversations before." His eyes flickered to the watcher, the small, black camera in the upper corner of his office. Every moment of our discussion would be added to the colony archives. You can't ever think you're alone down here. Then he looked at me hard, and I could tell he was going to choose his words carefully.

"So if anyone wanted to explore the Burn, they should be cautious, listen to good advice, but shouldn't believe false information. Now if you'll excuse me." He finally took a sip of his coffee, turned his back on me, and opened his computer. "Please shut the door on your way out."

TWO

"What is with you today?" Jessa asks as we leave Brant outside the Juice Deck. Jessa and I have to be home in seven minutes to help Grandma with dinner before Dad gets home from the colony offices at 18:00. We head to the nearest transport that will take us through the traveling tubes of the colony and drop us off in the living quarter.

There are more people in the corridors now, leaving their vocations for the day, leaving school, leaving their enrichment lessons. The corridor buzzes with people talking and laughing. I watch two boys a few years older than Jessa and me. They talk excitedly about some new variety of angler fish they had seen while exploring the Trench in their field studies. I've seen hundreds of angler fish before. Sure they have a bioluminescent dangler. Big deal. A lot of fish down this deep do. But I learned last week in Burn History that only one species up on the Burn can do it—*pyractomena borealis*. The firefly. It flies around when the sky turns dark and flashes its little light, glowing like a star.

"Seriously. What's up?" Jessa asks again. She's irritated now. I had completely zoned out on her. I shrug.

"Nothing."

"Yeah, I'll bet it's nothing. Is it because of Brant? I know you guys've been friends for so long. I didn't think going out would be a problem."

I shake my head, waving away the distraction. "Nah, not a big deal."

We turn the corner, and the doors to the transport are closing. We slip in as fast as we can. The doors hiss all the way shut, and a monotone, female voice announces, "Next destination: the living quarter."

There are mostly other kids around our age on the transport, coming home from vocations and school. My stomach lurches as the transport drops, heading down the transport tube toward the living quarter. The transport tubes are clear, so you can see everything speeding by. The tubes go between levels in the colony, so usually all you see are lots of wires and air ducts and flashing lights. But sometimes the tubes skim along the outer wall, so suddenly you're plunged into blackness with only the eerie artificial light to keep you company. I involuntarily lean into Jessa as we fly out next to the water.

"Do you think we've over-done the Juice Deck? We've been there for two dates already. But it was where we had our first kiss, so it *is* kinda special."

Jessa keeps talking, going on about dates and what the options are in the colony, but that memory of Mr. Klein has me thinking. That had been a year and a half ago, and I had completely forgotten the conversation. He had all but given me his blessing to find a way to explore the Burn. So there has to be a way to do it, and I am convinced he knows about it. If he is as fascinated with the Burn as I am, he will have found a way by now.

Then I remember when I had surprised him that day, and the way he hunched over that laptop. Protecting the monitor from the view of the watcher, I realize. I remember the guilty way he slammed it closed and jumped up when he knew someone was behind him. The answers are on that laptop, and I have to see it. But there is someone always watching. How can I access his computer without getting him or me into trouble?

"So what are you going to do about that red-head that's been eyeing you every day this week?" Jessa whispers behind her hand.

"You can't prove anything!"

Then I realize I'm not sure what she even asked me. I was so caught up in planning, that the first words I hear are accusations that aren't actually there. "Wait, what?"

She rolls her eyes. "Honestly, pull it together, Terra. This is getting ridiculous." She curls a lock of hair around her finger coyly. "I said, what are you going to do about the red-head?" And she inclines her head toward a boy standing a few feet away from us. He looks down at a book in his hand when I glance his way.

"Him?" I lower my voice when it comes out as a squeak. "Please, Jessa. Don't embarrass me again. You know I don't want to double with you and Brant."

"Oh, come on. He's kinda cute in a gangly sort of way. And besides there's the summer dance tomorrow night in the atrium. Everyone will be there. You skipped the past two years. I'm not letting you miss this one, too."

My mind churns ahead. Everyone will be there—they always are. It is a break in schedule. We don't have to be in our quarters, don't have to clock in at 22:00 for bed. It's an event that is probably tame for the Burn but almost borders on riotous for all of us down here. It is the perfect chance to slip to Mr. Klein's office without being seen.

"Okay." I try to seem casual.

Jessa looks at me like I've swallowed too much seawater. "Serious?"

"Yes."

"No way."

"Yes. Serious. I promise."

Jessa claps her hands, then promptly makes her way over to Red Head. His eyes flicker over to me a couple times, and the blush that creeps up his face turns the dusting of freckles across his cheeks dark red. Then a huge smile breaks out on his face. He comes over to stand in front of me, and holds out a hand that is mostly long, skinny fingers.

"I'm Matt."

I almost laugh but bite my tongue. No one down here is named Matt. Too common of a Burn name. Dad will love this.

"Terra."

"Hi, Terra. I'm glad to meet you. Do you want to go to the dance? Tomorrow night? With me?" He's unsure of himself as the questions come tumbling out. The transport lurches to a stop at the living quarter. We amble out.

"Sure, that'd be nice." I turn toward the corridor that leads to our house. He smiles.

"I'll come by at 7."

"Great." I hardly look at him. I hope that isn't too weird. But he must be fine with it, because he lopes off down another corridor.

Jessa bounces alongside me. "That was so perfect! This is going to be the best dance ever. I'll be with Brant, you'll actually come. Maybe I can convince Dad not to give another long, boring speech, and it *will* be the best dance ever."

The corridor is softly rounded so there are no corners and everything looks fluid. Front doors of quarters line the walls on either side of us, recessed a few feet by archways. Mr. Klein told me the Burn has similar living arrangements. They're called apartments.

We stop at ours and Jessa holds her palm to a white, glass panel to the right of the door. A light flashes across the surface of the glass, scanning her hand. Then the door slides open.

Our quarters have one big common room with a couch, desk, and multi-purpose monitor. There is a big window with a view of dark ocean. There are a few plants hanging from the ceiling. The kitchen and washroom arch off on one side, and the three bedrooms arch off on the other. Jessa throws her bag on the couch.

"Hey, Gram. We'd better be making something easy tonight because I want time to pick out dresses for us. This is going to be amazing!"

"Welcome home, girls," Grandma calls absently. She stands in front of the monitor. There is an image of a meal being prepared, and that same monotone female voice as the transport tube says, "Tuesday's nightly meal. Whole wheat macaroni and cheese with steamed vegetables and fish fillets. All nutritionally balanced for your health and perfectly seasoned for your taste.

20

You will find the ingredients have been delivered to your refrigeration unit. Please leave the monitor on while I guide you through the preparation."

Gram zooms in on a picture of the ingredients. She shakes her head. "Milk. So many of these meals have milk. I really ought to speak with the nutritionists. Surely they could design a meal schedule that includes milk-free options instead of just offering a supplement capsule. Last Wednesday's breakfast required milk, and now this one. It's hard when your father is lactose intolerant." She mumbles a minute more, then looks up and smiles. "Just in time to help."

Jessa flits into the kitchen. I sigh and drop my bag next to hers. I better get dinner over with so I can plot my deviousness that is scheduled to take place tomorrow night.

Gram measures out our prescribed servings of mac'n'cheese, and Jessa and I lay the forks and knives out when Dad walks through the door.

Dad is tall. He is taller than most of the colonists, and it helps his job as Speaker. He is physically imposing, and it is amazing how many people respect that. Sometimes people listen to him just because he is bigger than they are. I told Dad once that's what bullies do, and he laughed it off.

"But I don't bully them, Terra. They just talk themselves into feeling bullied. The last thing any of our colonies need is a bully. We're not like the Burn. We live off of unity, equitable compromises, and peaceable decisions."

Then suddenly the corners of his mouth fell and the creases around his eyes drooped and he went to his room for three hours. He only has one picture of my mom that he kept after she left. I've never seen it because he guards it like a treasure in his room. But sometimes I think he goes in there and talks to it.

Does it help, talking to her? He's the one who made her leave.

Dad puts his bag in the cubicle by the door. Then he reverently removes his Speaker's sash and hangs that next to the cubicle, carefully brushing out the wrinkles with his hands. Gram's eyes burn with pride as she watches her son take the proper care of his position that she taught him. I snort. But quietly, of course.

Dad sniffs the air. "That smells great, but my secretary told me it has milk in it tonight. She promised to speak with the nutritionists. We have diverse enough dietary needs that Food Prep really needs to make more specialized meals. Enough of this prescribed dinner for everyone."

I smirk. "But Dad, equity for all?"

It is a smart-aleck comment, and I know it. But I can't help myself. Gram eyes me icily, but luckily Dad doesn't catch the sarcasm.

"Equity doesn't always mean we all have the exact same thing. As long as we all receive the same nutrition to meet our needs, it is equitable. And I'd really love to eat something that didn't make me feel like vomiting."

He ruffles my hair. Since he won't be eating the mac'n'cheese, Gram sets his supplement capsule next to his veggies and fish.

"So, girls, tell me about your vocation today."

We spend a few minutes in idle chatter, me telling him the monotonous details of irrigation and Jessa more animatedly telling about pruning and then the Juice Deck with Brant. Then she goes in for the kill.

"And Terra's coming to the summer dance with me and Brant tomorrow night."

Dad almost shoots a piece of broccoli out his nose.

"Terra at the dance?" Gram says, bewildered.

Jessa nods, positively beaming. I show a sudden interest in my whole-wheat elbow noodles.

"Terra, is that true?" Gram asks.

I nod and put a big piece of fish in my mouth so I won't have to immediately answer any questions.

"Are you going with anyone?" Gram says. My dad still hasn't recovered and is coughing into a napkin.

I nod and chew slowly.

"That's wonderful. Isn't that wonderful?" she says. Dad's whole face is red, but he finally clears his throat.

"Yes, quite. Your mother would be pleased. Who are you going with?"

That is the question I've been dreading. I have no idea what to tell them about Matt.

"Umm, he's this kid, Matt, that Jessa and I met on the transport."

"Matt," Dad says, turning the name over in his head. He taps his chin. "Matt." He puts his fork down and leans back in his chair. "Uncommon name down here. What's his last name?"

I shrug. "Don't know."

"Is he your age?"

"Maybe a year or two older."

"What does he look like?"

"He's tall and skinny with red hair and freckles."

"Hmm. Red hair is pretty rare too. Think I'd remember that one. Maybe he's a recent transfer from another colony. I'll have to look into it."

I just about die. The last thing I need is my dad getting the file on the random guy I am using as a decoy on the night I am going to hack Mr. Klein's computer.

"Oh, please, Dad! My first date in I don't know how long, you don't need to call security on him."

Dad smiles, but it isn't all teasing. "Just looking out for you, Terra." He stabs another piece of fish and slowly puts it in his mouth.

Every word implies that I am the liability in the family. I am the rebel. I express the most interest in the Burn, I haven't found a vocation, and now I am going on a date with a mystery boy who doesn't seem to fit in. If only my dad knew how much of a rebel I am considering becoming. I spend the rest of the meal studying my plate.

THREE

Dad offers to clean up dinner, so Jessa and I make a dash for our room. When the door closes, Jessa throws herself at the closet.

"I can't believe the grilling Dad gave you. It's like he thinks you're some kind of deviant or something. What do you think of this?" She pulls an orange skirt out of the closet.

When Jessa started out, I almost expected to be able to open up to her about how I was feeling at the table. A stupid thought, I know, but still I want to talk to somebody about this "explore the Burn" madness. But with Jessa it's almost easier not to talk. She doesn't understand the insanity I'm experiencing, she just wants me close and is excited to be going to the dance with me tomorrow night. I love her for it.

Jessa hauls out every skirt and dress in our closet to find the perfect ensemble for the dance. After she choses a black skirt with a hot pink shirt, she turns her scrutiny on me.

"What are you going to wear?"

I lie on the bed, staring out the window. The ocean frowns back at me. I squint, straining my eyes for the surface that floats thousands of feet above me, hoping I can see some kind of light that isn't man-made. Then a light does appear faintly in the dark. Lazily, an angler fish swims into view, all teeth and blind eyes and the long, glowing dangler hanging down in front of its mouth.

That's what life is like down here. You hope for glimpses of light, and when you find it, you realize there's nothing there but a gaping mouth and sharp teeth and it'll swallow you whole if you aren't careful.

I throw a book at the window. It thumps against the borosilicate and the fish darts away. The light fades into the black.

Jessa sighs, long and dramatic.

"Sorry," I say. She raises an eyebrow. I drag myself away from the window. "No, really. Sorry. I've just been thinking about a lot."

Her eyes quiz me.

"I was just feeling like I . . . like I should go . . . " What am I doing? I can't tell any of this to Jessa. The watcher next to the window records all of this, and Jessa will be implicated.

"Like I need to change vocations," I finally stammer out.

"Again?"

I nod.

"Do you realize how many times you've changed?"

"Five. And you're the last person I need to remind me."

"Sorry. But someone needs to tell you. Again. I really thought we'd have fun on the field together. I was excited when Dad told me they thought farming would be a better fit—more light, more quiet time, helping something grow."

26

When she says it like that, farming does sound like a good fit. She's right—there is light. Practically identical to real sunlight except that it won't end in a supernova. That has to be better, right? Maybe I should try to like it. Maybe I'll go tonight and give it one last try. I probably don't have very many days left until my Burn exploration begins, so I better make sure I know what I'm doing.

Then she grows quiet. "And maybe you should stick with it for Dad."

I snort. "Yeah, right. Dad gives me as hard a time as he can. Why would I make it easier on him?"

Jessa is suddenly busy with her hair, not looking at me. "You know it's hard on him every time you do something like this. He just thinks he's a failure. That if Mom were still here, you'd be fine."

I sit electrified. I've noticed the way Dad cries, the way he consoles himself by talking to someone who will never talk back to him. But I'm hardly concerned. He brought it on himself. But then a sliver of guilt pricks my heart. Dad lets the grief eat himself from the inside out. The devil in me wants to tell her why he cries so much about it. But I can't.

I sit up. "You're right. I've got to go."

Jessa's eyes can meet mine again. "What? But what are you going to wear?"

"The red one's great," I say as I leave.

Dad looks over from the monitor as I make for the front door. Several other colony councilors are on the screen. He mutes the discussion.

"Where are you going?"

"Umm, just to the pod at Field #3. I left something there this afternoon."

"It can't wait until tomorrow?"

"No, it's important."

Dad checks his watch. "Okay, but be quick. You need to clock in for bed in forty-five minutes."

I nod and hurry out the door.

The corridors are quiet. Most colonists are inside for the night. A few stragglers come off the transport, and most of them eye me with surprise as I hurry by. They all know who I am, of course. Everyone knows who I am. My dad is the speaker, so there are countless times I've been seen with him at official functions. And I am a twin. That stands out in people's minds too. And my mother left us. That's the stain that nabs me the most glances. I can just imagine what people think. *We strive for peaceable living. So why did the speaker's wife run out on him?* If only they knew. It is a dirty secret I am too ashamed to tell. Maybe that's part of the reason I am so eager to get out of here. Too many secrets, too many things to hide. Too many times Dad tried to overcompensate for being the only parent. With the ocean pressing down on me, it feels like it could bury everything under its weight. The Burn feels more exposed—more honest.

The transport doors gape wide open and the transport is empty. This is the last transport back to the vocational quarter, and then one more transport back to the living quarter to arrive at 21:55, just in time for me to clock in before bed. I glance at my watch—perfectly synchronized with the clock on the transport—and tell myself not to miss it. I can't imagine how much trouble I'll be in if I don't make it home for curfew.

28

The door slides closed behind me, and the voice comes on, "Last transport to the vocational quarter. Upon exiting, you will have thirty minutes before the last transport leaves for the living quarter."

The transport jumps up the tube and whisks me toward the vocational quarter. I feel a rush of adrenaline. Pathetic, I know. But I've never been on this last transport. I gaze out the clear sides. The transport enters part of the tube that runs next to the ocean, and I stare at the blackness. Am I really considering leaving? Even though all this monotony is really grating on me, this is home. It is unchanging. Reliable.

And black. Much too black. Black surrounds me all the time. Sure the artificial lights cut through the dark, but if those go out, there would be nothing to guide me. One of the first things I learned when Dad was teaching me to use a submarine was to check and double check my instrumentation before undocking. If any of that failed when I was out in the Trench, I'd get so turned around that I'd be lost forever. I think about what Mr. Klein said in class once on a day we studied Burn navigation, that even on the darkest nights up on the Burn, you can use the stars to guide you. I wonder if he is the best man for what the councilors want to happen in Burn History classes. Mr. Klein makes it all sound so *hopeful*.

I press my hand to the glass, and wonder if there's anything to feel out there besides the empty cold. Then the tunnel burrows back into the colony, and all I can see is a blur of lights and machinery.

I get off by Field #1 and walk down the corridor to Field #3's pod. I put my hand on the scanner and the door hisses open.

There's a lot of security around here, though not a lot of violations. The founders were meticulous from the beginning. I am only given access to the field I am currently assigned to. That protects our food from kids who could just be goofing off or someone who is sleepwalking, I guess. No one comes down to the fields to goof off. There's nothing to do down here. And they can't get into one of the lockers to grab a radiation suit anyway, so they'd totally fry.

Which is kind of what I have in mind.

This plan of mine is stupid. I will march into the field with those solar lamps blazing and lie down among the corn and just try to catch a glimpse of what it might feel like to be up on the Burn. Just a peek. For just a minute. To see if it can be all I have been building it up to be in my head.

The importance of the solar radiation suit was the second lesson I learned when I switched vocations to agriculture. The first was how dangerous the solar lamps are. All of that overloads my brain as I walk toward the door that opens onto the field. But I don't hesitate. I need to do this. It is my last test to see if I really am ready to abandon all this.

The door opens too slowly.

"Let me out there." I realize I said it aloud. It's like the door gives me time to change my mind, but it's pointless. I squeeze out through the gap.

I gasp and feel my arms. I'm warm. Actually, truly warm. I glance at the temperature monitor on the wall. 85 degrees. I've never felt warm down here. Sure, under my covers at night, or after a shower. But never just walking down the corridor, or sitting in the Juice Deck—everything is too perfectly climatized.

Even our radiation suits are temperature controlled. A shiver of pleasure runs down my back. I walk into the corn.

I never realized how green the corn is. Through the filtered visor of the suit or the filtered plastic looking into the field, the corn is green, a dull grayish green that looks half alive. Now with naked eyes, this is vibrant and soft at the same time. The leaves shine under the artificial light. I have the wackiest urge to just touch the leaves. I do. They are smooth under my bare fingertips. The tassels on the ears of corn flutter in air currents swirled by the air circulators. The tassels feel fuzzy and ethereal. The soil is rich brown and smells alive. I never even knew dirt had a smell.

I kneel down between rows of corn, my bare hands in the dirt, my fingers raking through it. How long have I been in here? I look at my watch. Twenty minutes until the last transport. I will stay for five more minutes.

A trickle of sweat runs down my back. It's 85 degrees in here, and I never knew that was enough to make me sweat. With the added humidity, I feel deliciously slippery. My head feels tired and sluggish, and I lie down in the dirt, squinting up through the overlapping leaves of corn at the artificial lamps over head that I imagine are the sun.

Then the speaker crackles on. "The last transport leaves in five minutes."

I jump up. Did I actually fall asleep down here? I look around. I'm still alone, and I don't see anyone through the field's glass. No one knows I'm here. I look down at myself. I'm covered in dirt. I run to my locker and rip off my shirt and pants and change into the spares.

I bolt out into the corridor and jump onto the transport. There are two other people there, probably getting off cleaning shifts. One of them raises her eyebrows at me, but I shrug it off. Probably wondering what the daughter of the speaker is doing on a transport by herself so close to curfew. What have I been doing? I took a cat nap without a radiation suit lying on the dirt in Field #3. It sounds so crazy. But then I smile, remembering the warmth and the smells. The reddish light through my closed eyelids. Definitely not wasted time.

I make it back to my house at 21:57. Dad is still up, reading a bulletin. He doesn't look up when I come in.

"You're cutting it close, young lady. Next time you forget something and feel the need to go get it so close to—"

Then he looks up, shocked. My clothes are clean, so are my hands. He shouldn't be able to tell what I was doing. Then I notice my arms.

"Terra, you are bright red! What have you been doing?"

A burn? For only being on the field for maybe fifteen minutes? Could I really have a burn already?

"The only place you could have—" Dad clamps a hand to his mouth. "Were you out on the field without a suit on?"

I nod and hurry toward my room.

"If your mother could only see—"

"Well she can't, can she? Because you made her leave." Why am I doing this to him? Only an hour ago Jessa helped me realize how much Dad is hurting. But I can't stop; the momentum behind my words propels me on. "You really must have loved her to mess things up so badly."

Dad's mouth hangs open, and the tears surge up in his eyes. All I want from him is the truth. To set the ashes free from just one of the dirty secrets we all hide down here. To watch the remains of it fly on the wind and go rest somewhere in peace. The guilt claws at my stomach and I have to escape that look on his face.

"I've got to clock in." I turn my back on him and go to my room.

If I had known how agonizing sleeping in a bed would be with a sunburn, I would have stayed up and faced my dad's wrath, sorrow, and the punishment I will face from missing clock-in. Some time in the middle of the night, I wake up feeling like the skin is being peeled from my arms. Just having sheets on my burned skin is torture. I roll to one side, but my cheeks on the pillow aren't any better. A tear slips out, but the salt water running down my face is even worse than the bedding. I grit my teeth, sit up, and stay sitting up the rest of the night.

When Jessa wakes up, I'm already dressed and packing my bag for the day. She yawns and stretches, and then finally looks at me.

"Good grief, what happened to you?"

I shrug and try to keep the light fabric of my shirt away from my burned skin. "A few minutes on the field without a radiation suit."

"No way. For real?"

I nod. Her mouth opens in the wackiest smile I've seen on her.

"That's the dumbest thing I've ever heard. They just had another radiation suit reminder last week. How could you forget?"

"Don't tell Dad that. I'm already in enough trouble as it is." I go into the common room.

Dad waits in the kitchen, sitting in front of his egg white omelet with his hands on each side of the plate, palms down, like he holds the table steady to keep himself from chucking it at me. Or he could be holding himself together from the outside in. Gram eats her omelet in dainty bites. I sit at the table, and Dad gives her a look. She grabs her plate.

"I think I'll finish this in the other room while I get a sneak peek at lunch." She darts out into the common room. The monitor hums to life, but the volume isn't up very high. If I weren't in so much trouble, I would have laughed at Gram trying to eavesdrop on what's going on.

Dad doesn't waste any time.

"Terra, how could you be so completely thoughtless? So forgetful? So negligent? I know agriculture isn't your strong point and you're probably considering changing vocations again—"

I nod.

"—but I really wish you wouldn't be so reckless. You don't know how damaging those sun lamps can be."

I look at my skin. I have a pretty good idea.

"Why did you really go there anyway? I know you're not so idiotic as to forget a radiation suit. And don't tell me you forgot something. You wouldn't go out on the field just because you forgot something. I don't want excuses. That's not something anyone in this family would do. It's not something a daughter of a speaker would do." He finally takes a breath. I don't know what to say. I haven't thought ahead to come up with some excuse. Anything to save me from trouble.

Then Dad takes another deep breath. He brings his hands up and rubs his eyes. I know he will let it go. Then he looks at me.

34

"Speaking of vocation changes, considering your work record, I thought maybe it was time you made a change. Have you thought about trying public service?"

My temper flares. So that's it? I'm being groomed to be the next speaker? I was determined to keep my mouth shut, to be kind, but everything I've been feeling over the past few days comes spilling out before I can put a clamp on it.

"Really, Dad? Public service? You think I have any desire to be a speaker like you or Gram? I hate it down here, and if you knew anything about me, you'd know that. Why would I want to be an advocate for this stupid, messed up place? I'm very seriously considering following in Mom's footsteps, and I don't mean being a nutritionist."

I shouldn't have said it. That Mom comment goes way too far. But I have to tell someone what's rolling around in my head before it explodes, even if it is my dad.

He's horrified and looks like his nose has just been punched—his eyes water and his face is red. His mouth quivers, with sadness or rage, I don't know. I don't want to stick around to find out. I grab my bag and run out the door as fast as I can. He doesn't even have time to collect himself to tell me how much trouble I'm in.

FOUR

My feet pound down the corridor, and the only thing I can think about is my scorching skin. I need something for it, but I have no idea what to do for a sunburn. It's not something they teach us in first aid; it just doesn't happen down here. Well, except to neurotic teenage girls who are planning to defect.

I need to go to the infirmary, but I'm terrified of having to give a report. They'll observe me, they'll know what I did, and they'll call Dad in. Then we'll have round two of our bout this morning, and I'm too physically and emotionally exhausted to face him again.

Mr. Klein can help me. If anyone knows what to do, he will. He'll have studied sunburns, or at least know what can help it feel better. I get on the transport. I left early, without eating breakfast, so there are only a few people, and they're involved in catching up on messages, getting ready for their day. My hair is too short to cover everything, but I let it fall around my face to hide the redness.

The transport stops at the vocational quarter first. Then the doors close and the transport zooms along to the education quarter. The doors open and I get off in a circular foyer with corridors jutting off like wheel spokes.

There are more people down here, teachers preparing for classes, students who are on early schedule (they even schedule us according to our bodies' natural rhythms). I take the fifth corridor that holds the teacher's offices. I stop outside Mr. Klein's and hope he's there by now. I knock.

"Come in," says a muffled voice. The door slides open and I hear the click of his laptop closing.

He flips through a thick book laying open on the desk, and a cup of coffee is in his left hand. He hasn't looked back to see the monstrosity his prized pupil has become.

I clear my throat. "Um, Mr. Klein, I was wondering if you could help me?"

"Mmm," is all he says as he puts a bookmark between two pages, closes the book, and then glances up at me. He drops his coffee, spilling it all over the tile.

"Terra! What in the world?" He picks up his mug, then grabs the napkins that are neatly stacked on the edge of his desk. "Did you go out on the field without a suit?"

I nod, and I'm not ashamed in front of him. I felt mortified when faced by my dad, but I know Mr. Klein will understand.

He opens the small silver laundry chute and throws the napkins in it. His stack of napkins will be refreshed by this evening.

"I would ask why, but I think I know." He sits back down. He glances at the watcher, reminding me not to say anything out of turn. He clears his throat and laces his fingers together. I remember our conversation a year and a half ago. Once again, he will choose his words carefully.

"Nothing too serious that the infirmary needs to take a look at. I think that's why your father didn't send you there. I have something that will help that burn feel better." He stands up and I start leaving the office.

"No, no." He ushers me back in and motions me into his chair. He rolls it into position so I face his laptop and my back conceals it from the watcher.

"If you wanted to get started reading about what we're covering in class today, that would be great. I had it open before you came in. I'll be back in a few minutes."

Then he walks out and carefully shuts the door behind him. The lock slides automatically in place.

I turn to the laptop. There's something on here he wants me to see, and I have a feeling it's about escape. But as far as I know, Mr. Klein has never left the colony, and he doesn't seem the type to actually do it in the future. So what will I find on here? And then I realize I am here, where I wanted to be tonight, doing exactly what I wanted to do, and Mr. Klein has set it up so perfectly for me—he won't get in trouble and neither will I. My heart lurches.

I open the laptop and the screen flickers on. First glance: a messaging window and a list of past communications. They're all from someone named Gaea. The name sounds familiar. I've heard it recently, but where? Then the computer blips at me. The message window is still active. Mr. Klein was messaging with Gaea when I interrupted.

Rint. Are you still there?

My fingers hover over the keyboard, not sure what to do. Should I respond? Maybe Gaea is who I needed to talk to all along, and here is my chance. So why am I frozen in this position, my fingers inches from writing a message to this person?

If I do not hear from you in ten seconds, I will terminate our connection.

Ten seconds. Agony. My mind races, reaching out. Gaea. Who could it be? Someone in the colony? Surely not. Messaging connections are all routed through the watcher servers where they can be documented forever.

Nine. Who is Gaea? Think! No one has enough control to terminate a connection themselves. This is an independent connection. It has to be an outside source.

Eight. The name Gaea is from Mr. Klein's class. Someone ancient. Before modern Burn History.

Seven. A suspicious thought flutters into my head before I can even stop it. Would Mr. Klein set me up? And why would I even think such a dumb thing? So what do I type?

Six. Don't I want to escape this insane asylum? All these people whose lives are scheduled, meals are prescribed, recreation, exercise, . . .

Five . . . vocations all assigned to them. The field, the stupid corn field that is hell for me when it's my job, but a mystical, magical place when I'm not working and is burning my skin from my bones. The smell of the corn, the smell of the soil. Dirt. Earth. Gaea. Greek mythology. *The earth goddess.* Which, for Mr. Klein, translates into the Burn goddess.

Four. My fingers start typing before I even realize it.

Three.

Two.

One. I press *send.*

```
Not Rint. One of his students.
```

Agonizing, terrible silence as I wait for a response. Will she cut the connection when she realizes it isn't Mr. Klein? I close my eyes, mad at myself. Stupid. Always stupid. Admitting I'm not Mr. Klein. Acting and not thinking. Then the computer blips at me again. I open my eyes.

```
Terra?
```

I almost jump out of my seat. How does she know me?

```
How do you know my name?
I know all about you. Rint talks a lot.
Who are you?
Gaea.
Yeah, I know. The earth goddess. But what
does it mean?
From what Rint's told me, I think you're
smart enough to figure it out.
```

She's being forthright. Maybe I will be too.

```
I want to leave the colony. I want to go to
the Burn.
```

Just a second too long of a hesitation, but I suppose anyone would have that reaction.

```
I can help you if you're willing to make sacri-
fices. In the Trench. On the far side of the
observation station. On the east wall, look for
a fold in the rock. It hides the entrance to my
home. Tonight.
```

The message window goes blank and the screen says, "Connection terminated."

Then there's a whirring sound. Mr. Klein is on the other side of the door, his hand up against the scanner. I close the laptop and turn around in the chair. I give a furtive glance at the watcher. Did I stay in front of the screen well enough? My heart races. Will I leave tonight? Am I ready for that? I think so, but then why am I shaking?

The door slides open, and Mr. Klein carries a clear bottle. He holds it up.

"Aloe vera." He tosses it to me. "Rub some of that on your skin."

I squeeze some onto my palm and rub it on my burned arms and face. The goopy gel feels cool and tingly on my skin, and I sigh in relief.

"Just apply it every couple of hours. You aren't blistered, so you should be fine." Mr. Klein clears his throat. "Do you think today's lesson will be interesting?"

He's studying me, a look of worry etched in his eyes. I nod.

"Yeah, very. Thanks for letting me prep for it." I walk to the door. He stands to one side to let me pass.

"Are you going to the dance tonight, Terra?"

I turn around. Mr. Klein is sitting down and opening his laptop. This time he really does look at lesson plans, and he doesn't care if the watcher sees the screen or not.

"Um, yeah. Some guy I met on a transport asked me."

"That's good. Good you'll be out. Everyone will be out, you know. No after-hours vocations tonight. No farmers, no sanitation crew, no submarine dockers."

And I know instantly what he's telling me. If I'm going to meet with Gaea, if I'm ever going to leave for the Burn, tonight is my chance. If I'm serious about this, as Mr. Klein apparently hopes I am, this is it. No more dreaming, no more complaining about the colony. I have to act. This is what I've been looking for for so long. So why am I terrified?

I leave Mr. Klein's office. I need to be to class in twenty minutes, so I'm not in a hurry. Just chemistry and then Mr. Klein's class. Two hours that I know will stretch interminably.

I'm right. As soon as my chemistry teacher starts talking, my mind shuts off and my eyes drift to the map of the earth tacked to the wall behind her. The land is all shaded gray, and the oceans are shades of bright blue, a different shade for the territory of each colony. My colony, the Mariana colony, has the largest territory. Then I have a gut-wrenching thought.

Where am I going to go?

When I actually leave for the Burn, where will I go? It isn't labeled on the map, but I know the closest country is Japan. I don't speak Japanese. Everyone down here speaks English. "The language of science" had been the logic when everyone came down here in the beginning, without much other thought to what language they would use. The language of the colonies.

So what is it like on the Burn? Does everyone still speak their own languages? Did they choose one common language—the language of the survivors? Was it English? Will I be able to speak with anyone up there? I glance to the United States.

I could go to Hawaii. But it is such a remote island. Will there be anyone left? The mainland United States just looks so far away. How long will it take me to get there by myself? But do I have another option? I could go to Australia. But Australia wasn't very densely populated in the first place.

But why do I want to go up on the Burn in the first place? Is it for the freedom or for the people? I thought it was for freedom, but asking myself all these questions about languages and survivors, I realize I am just as hungry to experience my freedom *with* someone.

The United States then. Somewhere on the west coast. Anywhere on the west coast. I don't know too much about the United States—we haven't devoted much of our class time to its history yet. I've only learned bits and pieces of its history as it relates to other nations—so mostly economic and war facts. Periods of plenty followed by war and deep depressions. Are they in a depression now? Perhaps, I tell myself, but that's just the way nations' economies go. Where else would I go? Before WWIII, the United States took away all freedom of speech and personal privacy in a dramatic attempt to eradicate terrorism. They had watchers in every classroom, every home. There was even a bill in congress for personal identification implants so the government could always track their citizens' movements. Too much like down here, that voice in my head says again. But where else can I go? The United States dropped the first nuclear warhead that began the Event. I shudder, but silence the voice. There isn't anywhere else to go. And if I keep this debate up, I'll scare myself into staying home. Forever.

My head is still awhirl when my class is dismissed, and I gather my things without realizing what I'm doing. I walk past the other students, probably bumping into some—I don't remember—on my way to Mr. Klein's class.

He doesn't say anything to me when I walk in, so I assume he doesn't even look up. I'm not paying attention. I just sit in the first available desk and stare at the wall in front of me as Mr.

Klein begins his discussion. The kid next to me leans over and hisses a whisper.

"Did you catch that last date?"

I stare straight ahead. I'll leave tonight and never come back.

"Hey, Terra, did you hear me? The last date?"

I'll go somewhere I've never been before.

"Are you even listening?"

I won't know anyone. I'll have no friends.

"Whatever."

Am I sure I want to do this? It would be easier just to stay home.

I shake my head. I need to focus, pay more attention. Letting my thoughts wander like this will get me into trouble. I know what I want. I've known it for a long time, and I won't let my fears talk me out of it.

I remember Gaea's words: I can help you if you're willing to make sacrifices. In the Trench. On the far side of the observation station. On the east wall, look for a fold in the rock. It hides the entrance to my home. Tonight.

FIVE

I rub aloe on my arms as I watch Jessa put the last touches on the maze of curls and braids she has transformed her hair into. It took her an hour to do her hair. Jessa isn't usually high maintenance, but she is willing to spend time on her hair. It's 18:20, and Matt and Brant will be here in forty minutes. Jessa is already in her skirt and top, but my stomach keeps flipping and my hands shake as I try to zip up my red dress, making putting on the flimsy piece of fabric nearly impossible.

I growl in frustration as my unsteady hands slip from the zipper again. Jessa does it for me.

"Seriously, Terra, calm down. Take a deep breath or something. I know this is your first date in a while, but you'll be fine. Really."

I give her a weak smile. Just let her think that's what is giving me anxiety. It's the easiest explanation I can offer her. Then she snags my hand as she pulls away from the zipper, and she looks into my eyes. Her face—like looking into a reflection, except for the slightly upturned nose, the narrower chin—is so like mine. But we are so completely different, and I'll miss it. My throat catches with a sudden ache as I think of leaving her forever. Her green eyes continue to bore into mine with a stare that becomes too perceptive. I slip into my shoes.

"You doing alright?" she asks, still holding my hand. "You don't have to do this, you know."

If I didn't know better, I would have thought she is talking about my leaving. And I almost shout out, "Yes I do! And you can come with me!"

What will I do without her? And what will her life be like without me? Will she miss me? Will she just go off with Brant and live happily ever after? I hope so because she belongs here. I'm selfish to think of taking her with me. I catch her up in a fierce embrace.

"Love you, Jessa. Always have."

She laughs. "Love you, too." Then she pulls back and looks at me again, the laugh still playing with her mouth. "You're weird."

I make a face at her and turn so she can't see my eyes full of tears. She slips a few sparkling barrettes into my hair.

Gram knocks on the door. Then I hear her giggle. Giggle? Gram? Jessa and I look at each other. I didn't know Gram could giggle. Jessa opens the door.

Gram sweeps her arms open for a double hug. Gram smells of freesia and nutritionally optimized bread slices, and I breathe it in deeply. She pats my head.

"You both look lovely. I'm thrilled you're going together. I'll be there for a little while, at least, and I'm excited to watch you dance."

I look at her clothes then, and she's dressed up too, and her hair is neatly combed into soft, silver curls around her face. She beams at us.

I will have to stay at the dance long enough to convince Gram I'm having a good time and would dance all night long if I could. I squeeze her hand and give her a quick kiss on the cheek.

"Oh, and Terra. Matt's here already."

I freeze. He's five minutes early. I haven't prepared myself for this. I had thought and rethought what to pack, the quickest route to the submarine dock, what I will say if I run into someone along the way. But it hadn't crossed my mind what I will actually do with this boy tonight. Gram turns to go out into the common room, and Jessa grabs my arm when it looks like I'm not going to follow her.

"He's just a guy, Terra," she says. "Calm down."

I let her lead me into the room.

Matt stands next to the door, and he has a rose in his hand. A flower? I don't even know his last name, and he's giving me a flower on our first date. He holds it out to me. Then he notices my lobster skin and stutters.

"Y-y-you look nice," he says, as I take the flower. Gram bustles around finding a vase for it.

"Thanks." I glare at him. Why is he so nice to me? I'm just going to ditch him in a few hours. He looks down.

"Do you want to go already, or do you want to wait for your sister?"

"Um, let's wait for Jessa and Brant."

He can't think of anything else to say, and the look on my face tells him there isn't anything else to say, so he just rubs the toe of his shoe on the back of his pant leg and waits.

Awkward. Completely, totally awkward. And why not? Why should the last night of my life in the colony be any different from any other day I've spent here?

There is a knock at the door and Jessa opens it for Brant. He offers her a carnation and she throws her arms around his neck and kisses him. Dad comes out of his room and clears his throat. Jessa pulls back.

"Well, you all behave yourselves, and I'll see you there in a little bit."

That is all he says, and I raise my eyebrows, expecting more. Matt must too because he avoids my dad's eyes and blushes until the tips of his ears are bright red. But if this is the extent of Dad's words of wisdom for the evening, I'm definitely going to take it. But then he grabs my arm as we walk through the door.

"But don't think I'm done with you yet, young lady." His voice is a whisper. "I feel like you're dangerously close to doing something stupid, and I don't want to lose you. Just like your mother, regardless of what you think about that situation. We're having a long chat tomorrow during your personal reflection time. Got it?" He does his best to keep his face composed, but his eyes still shine.

I nod. There won't be a tomorrow.

The dance is in the atrium every year. The atrium is a large gallery next to the main submarine dock. The colony council gathers here to welcome people visiting from other colonies, as well as holds colony meetings and celebrations. It's a large bubble of borosilicate separated from the main colony by a tunnel. A single metal stilt plunged into the ocean floor supports the bubble, and a glass floor cuts the bubble in half, so it looks like you're suspended in the middle of the ocean in an air bubble. The effect is pretty spectacular—if you don't have issues with the black ocean crushing everything in sight.

Loud music plays through the dim lights. People swirl and sway to the music. It all melts into a blur of movement, color, and sound as Jessa and Brant lead the way into the middle of the bubble and join the rhythm of the couples dancing around us.

Matt dances next to me, his long, skinny arm bumping my shoulder as we move in contrary directions. He tries to stay near me as I try to make more room for myself. He brushes my hand as I take it away and cup it to my mouth to whisper some made-up secret to Jessa. She watches with a bemused smirk on her face. I should never have talked myself into this, thinking it a brilliant excuse for a chance to leave the colony. Is it worth this?

I imagine what one of the fish down here would see, if they weren't blind. A bubble floating through the ocean, filled with people moving to some unknown command, smiles on their faces, all flash and color, but nowhere to go. There would never be a change, it would always be stagnant. Just the same, eternal bubble floating with the same music, the same conversations, the same people.

Then the music stops, and the ebb and rise of the dancing stops, and we all turn to the podium. Dad makes his way up there to give his traditional Summer Dance Speech, and already the applause ripples across the crowd. I lean toward Matt, and he eats up this first show of wanting contact.

"I'm going to go get a drink."

He leans away, disappointed. But he rallies. "Would you like me to get it for you?"

"That's okay." I'm already walking away. "I heard my dad practicing this earlier. But you should stay and listen, it's great."

The crowd parts regretfully for me. *No one should miss this,* they seem to say. *This is the summer dance, the highlight of our year. Stay! Stay!*

But if this is the highlight, what does that say about all the rest of it? I feel a tug on my dress.

"Terra!" Jessa's there, with her hands on her hips. "What do you think you're doing?"

I swallow, looking around. Has it been that obvious what my plan was all along? I panic and my throat dries up.

"Thirsty."

"I don't mean about that. I mean with Matt. Can't you see he's totally bonked for you, and you're blowing him off. What's the deal?"

I look at her helplessly. What can I say? *Yeah, I know, I just came so I could run away without anyone stopping me anytime soon.* But it can only go two ways: Jessa will laugh at me, or she'll try to stop me with everything she's worth. And I can't gamble with those odds. So I just shrug my shoulders.

"I'm taking a quick break. You know, getting a drink and regrouping. I'm trying, Jessa, really I am."

Jessa relaxes. "Yeah, alright. I'm sorry. I'm just really determined to have tonight be fun for both of us."

She always wants everything to be fun for me. I hug her again, and I know it will be the last time.

"Thanks, Jessa. For everything."

"Wow, don't over do it," she says, laughing. She turns to go back to Brant and Matt. "I'll see you later."

I can barely nod.

My dad's voice echoes off all the hard surfaces of the bubble as I leave and wind my way through the corridors. There are watchers everywhere, and they record my every step, but it won't mean anything until it is too late. Everyone is behind me. Once they realize I'm gone they'll comb through the archives to follow me on my path through this corridor, along the transport that takes me to the vocation quarter, through three more corridors to the research submarine dock. They will see my panicked, determined, terrified, elated face as I sigh in relief that it is vacant.

Dad will no doubt watch as I walk to the single-man submarine bobbing gently in the water, moored by the robotic arm that provides both its power and diagnostic reports. Dad will watch this part for sure, and I ache for his grief—grief that I have helped linger. So I look around for the closest watcher. I turn to it so it can see my whole face.

"I love you. I love you all," I say before I get in the sub and turn my back on the colony forever.

SIX

I was trained to use a submarine since I could walk, and it's second nature to release the robotic arm, turn on the engines, slip from the dock into the black water, turn on the navigation system, and direct the sub toward the Trench.

The hard part will be finding Gaea's home. I have only been down the Trench a handful of times on class field trips or when Dad wanted me to come with him on official business. I'm not too familiar with the geography of things down there. I can get to the research station no problem, but as far as lips of rock that might hold houses, I have no idea what to look for.

The Trench looms ahead of me, and I slow down. With the sub's lights, I can see about twenty feet in front of me and the rest of it is pitch black. I could use the navigation system that shows where the sub is on a topographical map of the area. I glance at it once or twice, but I prefer to use what my eyes can see. I don't want to miss the edge of the Trench that will guide me down to the research station.

I float along slowly for a few moments, and then the bottom of the ocean, grayish in the lights from my sub, disappear and there is nothing but water. I descend down into the Trench.

I know it doesn't bother the researchers that come down here every day and often spend a week or two at a time in the research station. But every time I go down the Trench and watch the numbers on the gauge slowly drop to depths that would crush me if there was the tiniest flaw in my sub, I'm unnerved. I grip the controls tighter, and my knuckles whiten. I breathe deeply. This is all just part of it—part of leaving. It's not going to be easy. That's one thing Dad always told me—and I actually agree with him—"Anything worth having is never easy." The first time he told me this, I thought it was all just part of his political garbage, but he's right. He's right more than I give him credit for.

The depth gauge reads 34,224 feet. The deepest part of the Trench is still another 2,000 feet down, but I'm almost to the research station. There shouldn't be anyone here tonight—they should all have left this afternoon (or not even gone in at all) to be ready for the dance.

The station is dark. Just a few pricks of light shine through the darkness—the dock illuminators. The station is eerie in the darkness. Usually you can see the researchers through the well-lit windows, bustling about with their experiments. But the station is just an empty shell tonight.

Beyond the station, the lights of my sub catch the first waver of the warm water and smoke that fill this part of the Trench. The black smokers are thick here—hydrothermal vents that spew out sea water that seeps down into the earth and chars itself on the molten core. The minerals that escape back into the

53

ocean with the hot water form layer upon layer into huge chimneys. The water down here can get up to 500 degrees. That's one of the reasons the station is down here: to study the vents and the organisms that can live in these conditions.

There is a forest of the black smokers south of the station, some of them forty feet tall. Surely this is where Gaea's home is hidden. Somewhere along the east wall where the lip of rock, the smokers, the darkness, and the murky water will hide it unless you know it's there.

I start just south of the station and study the wall as high as the highest smoker here, down to where my lights no longer illuminate the wall. The wall of the Trench is irregular, but smooth, like the way a ribbon ripples in the air but is still satiny. The lights from the sub bounce off these ripples and make shadows. I think the first three shadows I see are the lip of rock Gaea's home hides behind, until I look closer and realize my mistake. It will take me hours to find her home like this. It has to be different. None of these ripples can hide an entrance that a sub could squeeze through.

I change the angle of the sub. Instead of facing the wall straight on, I am now at a 45 degree angle, facing southeast. I start combing the wall again.

There, just up ahead. There is a mouth of shadow that gapes open. I turn the sub full-face on it, and the darkness shifts to look like any of the other shadows threading its way up toward the abyssal plain. This has to be it.

I squint at the shadow mouth through the light. It's hard to differentiate what is rock and what is mere darkness. I inch forward and see the slightest variance between the shadows—one looks more ghostly, less substantial than the other. I follow the ghost.

The tunnel leads behind the lip of rock and then turns sharply to the left and up a steep climb. I follow it for five hundred feet before the tunnel in front of me disappears and the lights of the sub hit rock. This rock is more jagged. Even the slight ocean currents haven't made their way into this long tunnel to wear at the rock. This is closer to what it might have been when it was made.

But where now? The topographical map says there is nowhere else to go. I lean forward to peer up through the glass. I smile. There is a sub dock right above me.

When I open the top hatch, light streams into my eyes. Not strong light, just enough to illuminate everything around me. I'm in a small room filled with shelves of supplies—tins and pouches of food, first-aid supplies, folded clothes in neat stacks, shoes, tools, and other random odds and ends. An air filter chugs in one corner, its intake tubes reaching up and burrowing through the rock ceiling. There must be some kind of natural air pocket up there.

There is a door up ahead, the heavy kind that is on one of the larger subs. It's mounted to the rock wall. Light streams through the chinks between rock and door. Not the wild lights of the dance, or the pallid, white lights all around the colony, but warm yellowish lights that almost feel like sunshine if they had just been warmer. I hear voices on the other side—a jumble of voices that changes every few seconds. Men, women, children all talking over each other in muted tones. Who is on the other side of that door?

I creep forward, ignoring the scritch-scratch my shoes make on the rock. Gaea might be expecting me, but I still don't know what to expect from her, and I don't want her surprising me.

Before I heft the door open, I want a clue of what I'm up against. I look around the door and see a gap between it and the rock just wide enough for me to peek through. I lean my cheek against the damp rock and peer through.

My eyes adjust for a second. The lights are brilliant and warm. I blink. The wall to the left of the door is completely devoted to a bank of probably thirty different monitors, all showing different images. That is where the voices come from. The people on those monitors talk to each other or to no one in particular. All the images are from the same angle—just barely off from directly overhead. Some of the monitors show image after image changing in rapid succession, and others stay focused for minutes at a time. Sitting on a simple metal folding chair in front of the monitors is a woman with black hair streaked with gray that reaches out in wild waves all the way down her back. She hunches over to see some of the lower monitors, so from where I am, she looks like an indistinct lump. Then she turns to the door and stares hard at it with sharp, green eyes. I jump back.

"Don't just stand there staring. Come in."

I heave the door open. It scrapes along a groove worn into the rock from the door being pulled open and closed time and time again.

Gaea stands when I come in, and the indistinct shape falls from her to reveal a tall, slender woman. She wears a long colorful skirt, scuffed boots, and a loose shirt with long sleeves. A head band keeps her unruly hair from her face and makes the

56

hair around the crown of her head look like a black and gray halo. Huge earrings in the shape of elephants weigh down her earlobes. She has smooth, copper skin with furrowed wrinkles at her eyes and around her mouth. She smiles at me, and the smile is a dare to go through with what I have been contemplating for I don't know how long.

"So, Terra."

Gaea gestures to a chair in a corner of the room. I've never seen a chair like it before. It's woven out of some kind of wood. I run my fingers over it.

"Wicker." Gaea has a mocking smirk on her mouth. "Used to be a popular kind of furniture on the Burn."

It creaks at me as I sit down. I rub my palms on the arm rests.

"How did you get it?" I ask, the question I have for just about everything I see around me.

"I brought it here," she says, shrugging her shoulders. She goes over to the other corner of the room. There's a bed there—a mattress shoved into a recess of rock—and a dresser. A photo stands on one end of the dresser, but she turns it over before I can see it and tucks it under her pillow. Then she grabs a whistling tea pot off a burner.

"Coffee?"

"Real coffee, the kind with caffeine?" Has Mr. Klein been here to have real coffee?

Gaea takes two mugs from a drawer and pours a packet of dark crystals into each one. "The only kind of coffee. That garbage in the colony shouldn't be called coffee. Rint loves this. He requests it every time he comes to see me."

I have the feeling she is the kind of person I shouldn't ask too many questions of, but I can't help myself.

"Does he come here a lot?"

She hands me a cup and sits down on the folding chair. I'm about to take a sip when she stops me.

"Careful, you'll burn your tongue clean off." An odd glint comes into her eyes, but she tempers it and looks back at me with a shrug. "No temperature regulators."

I watch as she blows into her cup. "And yes, Rint comes when he can. Though his visits have been fewer lately. He and I were anticipating you."

"What do you mean?" Her presence is . . . I can't find a word for it. Almost ominous, like a bad omen. Of course that stuff is all bogus Burn superstition, but I feel like it applies perfectly to her.

I blow on my coffee, watching the small ripples float across the surface and then hit the edge of the cup. I take a sip and make a face. It is strong and bitter. I've never had coffee—even in the colony—and I wonder what all the fuss is about. Gaea laughs, a short rasping sound in her throat.

"We wondered when you would finally want to escape badly enough. So we limited our contact with each other. We didn't want anyone getting suspicious and stopping you."

"Um, that was good of you." I shift my weight uncomfortably. How many other people noticed I was itching to leave?

Gaea leans forward and puts a cold hand on my arm.

"Don't worry, all three of us have done our jobs well. I don't believe anyone knows you're here." She smiles, her pink lips parting over white teeth.

"But they'll know I'm gone soon."

"Of course," Gaea says, straightening up and the smile ebbing. "And they'll be searching the territory once they see you're no longer in the colony, and that will make getting to the Burn very difficult."

She sets down her mug and turns to the monitors. She pulls a computer keyboard off one of them and sets it on her lap. She clacks a few keys and the images on the screens begin to change.

"Where're you going?"

"The United States somewhere, I guess." I watch the monitors and try to see some pattern to the images there. Gaea looks at one and shakes her head, types a few words and the image changes. She does this over and over.

"Not what it's now called, of course. But New America may be a wise choice, given the current global climate."

"The current climate?"

She smiles that unnerving, smirking smile. "Not weather, of course. Politically. New America is the most stable nation at the moment. Though that's nothing to brag about, given the way they're enforcing the stability. Their citizens are required to live in designated cities. Anyone found outside is incarcerated in a labor camp. So many other nations broke out into civil war after the Event and war with each other as well. I suppose the relative peace in New America is admirable, but I wouldn't ask its citizens about it. You'd think something like this would have brought everyone together, but sadly it didn't. Too much finger pointing, too much 'I told you so'."

"How long have you been down here?"

Gaea's eyes flash to mine, something suddenly shrouding the bitterness that sits so openly there. She looks back to the monitors.

59

"A good while."

There's something she doesn't want to tell me. She turns her back, physically blocking any more questions. The images on the monitors slow as she seems to be happy with what she's seeing.

"Where do these pictures come from?" I ask, waving my hand at the monitors.

"Satellite images. Quite a few countries put up satellites for several years before the Event. And you thought the colony was the only one capable of invading people's privacy? Bah! The Burn isn't the bliss you've conjured up in that head of yours, Terra. They used these satellites as a way to watch people, track movements, try to subdue terrorism and other dangerous activity. And now I'm using them to keep tabs on what goes on up there. I have twenty-eight monitors, but there's probably two thousand or more satellites floating around in space. But these are the only monitors I could get."

"Mr. Klein?"

Gaea is remiss to divulge all her secrets to me, but she answers. "Yes, when those wasteful self-righteous . . . never mind. When there's extras, he tries to get them for me."

"No wonder he knows so much about the Burn." I gaze at the images on the screens. Five of the screens focus on various angles of rocky beach with brown-green water pounding the shore. Skeletons of buildings huddle under the sky. It is raining at this place, and a gray mist settles over the rocks. I've been longing for the sun, but even this looks magical.

"The Washington coast." Gaea gestures at the monitors. "I was thinking perhaps Arizona, but someone soft from the colony wouldn't last two days this time of year. Washington was one of the United States. Now there is only the federal government and all states have been dissolved, and they're calling themselves New America. This may be a good place to start. Bigger coast cities like Los Angeles and San Francisco were heavily targeted by the bombs and obliterated, and I haven't been able to see many survivors. But there seems to be more in this area. There will be shelter among the trees, and lots of wildlife."

I snap my head up. "Wildlife?"

I hadn't thought about the animals that may be out there. There will be animals that could kill me if they wanted to.

The corner of Gaea's mouth raises up. "Yes, wildlife, but what is that to a daughter of a man? Shouldn't man subdue all the beasts? But not to worry. I'll give you a few weapons. And if you're smart, you'll find a group of survivors quickly and figure out a way to make them trust you. It's summer, so they should be out instead of hunkered down to outlast the winter."

My stomach clenches up. What am I getting myself into? But Gaea doesn't give me much time for introspection. She pulls a map off of a shelf and spreads it out on the floor.

"This is Washington. You see the way the ocean cuts into the land here?"

I nod.

"You'll follow that and then down here to what's called the Puget Sound. You can land anywhere along here. I don't know if I'd go for the city of Seattle right away. It's a designated city for the citizens and you need to get a feel for the area and any hostilities."

"Hostilities? Is it still a war zone?" I am more nervous with every minute of this conversation.

61

"Were you expecting all sunshine and daisies? I think you'll find that most people will be hostile toward a stranger. And you are a stranger. We've been down here for a hundred years, and things will be very different for you up there. And there's general anger and distrust of things that are unknown."

"Do they know about the colonies? Is that why?" I rock back on my heels and wrap my arms around my legs. Despite the warmth from the lights, I start to feel cold.

Gaea's eyes glimmer with shards of light. "Yes, they know. They realized what was going on just before the Event. I don't blame them for being angry that all the best minds abandoned them—more or less left them with little hope of sorting things out on their own. That was one of the things that escalated the conflict. Though you won't find your father ever telling anyone that."

She spits the word *father* with such vehemence that I shudder. Once again her eyes cloud over. She continues as if nothing happened.

"They hate us for it."

"Oh." I want to escape the colony for a world where I may be eaten by an animal and everyone will most likely hate me. Gaea notices my sudden quiet and reaches out a long, slender hand on my own. Her skin is dark on my white. Just like Jessa's skin. The sudden reminder of my sister brings tears.

"It's okay, I was just thinking about my sister. Can I ever come back?"

"Out of the question. I'll program your sub to return here after you land. It would be too dangerous for everyone down here for people up there to come. They're too angry. Right now there isn't a way for the people on the Burn to find us, but there will be some day and I think it's best not to speed that up, but to let it happen by itself."

Why does she want to protect the colonies? Gaea stands up, brushing off her skirt. She motions me up. She turns on a burner like we use in chemistry and puts something metal on it.

"Which reminds me. There's one promise you have to make."

"Promise?" I remember what she said on the computer. Sacrifice.

"You can never speak of the colonies to anyone up there. Ever."

"Where do I tell them I come from?"

"You'll have to make something up, something believable. But if you love your sister and want to protect her, you can't ever speak of us. There hasn't been enough time between the Event and the present. Emotions are still too raw. If they knew there was a colonist among them, knew that you could somehow take them here, things will be so much worse for you and for us. Do you understand?"

Never speak of this life to anyone? Never even mention Jessa? Those are the memories I prize most—memories with her, doing nothing, talking, singing, laughing. The only fun I ever managed to have in the colony was with her. Because of her. And now that part of me will be buried forever.

"Terra, do you understand?"

Gaea has a look of knowing in her eyes, and my temper flares. How can she know what I feel?

But I bring the anger to a simmer and I nod. I will bury the feelings for Jessa, the longing and sadness deep in a grave in my heart and leave those skeletons there for always.

"Not a problem."

Then Gaea reaches over to a table by the monitors and faces me with a gleaming scalpel.

"I don't think you understand, Terra. You will be *unable* to speak of the colonies. Open your mouth."

My jaw clenches. I fall over myself and scrabble along the floor. Now I seriously doubt Gaea's sanity and her ability to help me. My mouth runs dry as she stalks me with the scalpel held by white knuckles.

"That's the only way?" I choke out, never taking my eyes off the sharp blade.

"I think your sister is the most precious thing to you. What would you do if you accidentally gave her away? If you were sleeping one night and spoke out in dreams of her at the bottom of the sea? If those sleeping by you heard such a thing? Would you risk Jessa that way?"

I stop at the door. This is the sacrifice she wants me to make. She must have dreamed of it all along. This is the price I will pay to earn my way to the Burn and protect the colonies. To protect Jessa. To seal her away forever. My dad's words come floating to me again. "Anything worth having is never easy."

I stand up, taking an hour-long minute to straighten my knees and shoulders and look Gaea in the face.

"Fine."

Gaea's green eyes bore into mine, and they flash once as they look for any trace of—what? Regret? She will find that etched all over me. Or maybe deception. To know that I can keep everyone down here a secret. Or maybe certainty. To know that this is what I want. Whatever she finds on my face leaves her satisfied, and she motions for me to sit on the wicker chair again, next to the burner. The metal piece on it shimmers in the heat.

"Now that's settled," she says, wrenching open the door to the supply room. She rustles for a few moments in there, and comes back with a syringe and a vial. She smiles condescendingly at me.

"I'm not a complete witch, you know. I will give you a little anesthetic." She stabs the needle into the vial and pulls back on the plunger. "Now open your mouth."

The moment of hesitation grips me before I can steel myself. I freeze to the chair, icy fear seizing my muscles into paralysis. Gaea clucks her tongue.

"A tongue is a small price to pay for your dream, isn't it?"

My tongue is the only muscle I can move. "What will I do up there if I can't talk to anyone?"

Gaea rubs down the scalpel with a disinfecting wipe. She shrugs her shoulders. "My dear, you have a lovely face and a lovely figure. You have very expressive eyes. You'll do just fine."

She tosses the wipe on the floor and steps closer to me with the scalpel in one hand and the syringe in the other. The burning in my stomach moves to my chest, and suddenly I can move my arms. But still they grip the arms of the chair. She binds me with her logic and my burning need to leave the colony.

"Now open your mouth."

Slowly I unclench my jaw and open it just a fraction. Gaea chuckles.

"That will never do. Do you want me to wrench it open for you?"

I open the rest of the way, and Gaea pricks the needle into the top of my tongue at the back of my mouth. I wince at the sting. Then she pricks with the needle again and again around my tongue, numbing the whole area. By the time she's done, I can't feel anything. She puts the syringe on the dresser and pulls a white towel from a drawer and holds it under my mouth.

"There will be quite a bit of blood, so keep your mouth open wide as you can. I'll cauterize the wound as soon as I'm done."

Did she say cauterize?

"Are you ready? Relax, dear, you won't feel a thing."

Then she puts the scalpel in my mouth. The bitter, metallic taste of blood floods my mouth and I choke. She turns from me quickly, my tongue dangling from her right hand, and grabs the hot metal piece from the burner. I open my mouth wider—I don't want that searing metal to touch anything more than my bloody stump. Gaea presses it in with a hiss, and a wisp of smoke curls from my mouth. I smell burning flesh and gag. Gaea pulls the metal out quickly, and I retch all over her floor. I look up, and tears glitter in her eyes.

Why is she crying? She intimidated me so much, why the moment of vulnerability? She smears a tear away with the blood-stained towel and the moment disappears like shadows.

"Now then, that should do it." She hands me a pill. "An antibiotic. Mouth wounds do heal quickly, but we want to be safe, don't we?" She turns and walks through the door.

I roll my stub of a tongue around in my mouth. I can't reach the roof of my mouth anymore, only the soft palate. The bitter blood taste washes away with the water I drink for the antibiotic.

Gaea refuses to look at me as she grabs a backpack off a shelf and shoves supplies in it, rattling off names as she goes. I struggle to keep up with it all.

"Sunscreen—be sure to put it on, especially with your skin tone. I see you've already had a bout of UV exposure, and it's not any better up there. MREs—you eat these—blanket, first aid kit, flint and steel wool—for lighting fires—a knife," she holds up a large, mean-looking knife, then sheathes it and puts it in the pack. "You'll probably want to carry that on your belt. Let's see here, what size?" Then she rifles through the stacks of clothes until she finds a few things that will fit me. She eyes my dress. "You'll definitely want to put these on before you land."

She puts the pack into my trembling hands, and I follow her numbly back to the sub dock.

"I think that should be all you need to start." She bends, her skirt pooling around her feet in brilliant colors, and opens the hatch.

I'm halfway down the ladder when she speaks, a heaviness in her voice that almost forces me the rest of the way down the hatch.

"You will never speak of us, Terra. But don't forget us."

Her eyes fill with tears again, but not just of sadness. There's also a triumph there. And suddenly those eyes look so familiar to me. But I must be going wonkers with all the pressure on me now. So I just nod and close the hatch behind me.

SEVEN

I don't notice the absence of my tongue in the sub. There's no one to talk to, and I'm not going to pick up Dad's habit of talking to someone who isn't there. I look at the coordinates Gaea programmed into my sub. It will take two days to reach the Washington coast and then just a few hours to maneuver through the waters into the Puget Sound.

Two days to myself aboard a claustrophobic sub. The thoughts of loneliness press like fingers into my brain. I close my eyes and breathe deeply to keep myself from screaming.

The sub follows the trench north through the system of canyons that are used for navigating this territory. At the precise latitude, it will ascend and go straight east toward Washington. After gazing through the window at nothing and studying the monitors until my eyes are fuzzy and dry, my body aches with tiredness. I'm hunched over the controls, tracking each mile of endless progress, and feel like my mind is on the verge of shutting off.

I need sleep. I didn't sleep well the night before, and now it's five o'clock in the morning. I lie down on the bunk that lines one side of the sub but my eyes feel wired open. I force them shut, and behind my lids all I see are forests, rain, rocky beaches. Over and over these images flash, faster and faster as they count down to a future that just might explode in my face.

The Burn. Most often I picture the desolation the colony has fed me—deserts, crumbling buildings, the blazing sun. But I saw beauty on Gaea's monitors. Maybe I will belong up there and it won't just be this childish fantasy I always dream of. It will be real, and I can touch it and feel it.

I fall asleep after my mind stops racing along faster than my body can keep up with. I wake up when the computer announces, "Now leaving the Northwest Pacific Territory. Entering the Northeast Pacific Territory."

I look at the clock. 18:00. I slept for thirteen hours. I again sit in the controller's seat. Just a few more miles and I'll pass Hawaii. That is the half-way point between my old life and my new.

Just as I pass it, the monitor blips at me, indicating a message is waiting for me. Surely Gaea wouldn't risk transmitting a message. Mr. Klein? But he can't let anyone know he knows where I am.

It is from Jessa. Should I even be tempted by this? I need to entomb this part of me to have a chance of happiness on the Burn. But my heart aches for one last piece of her. I press a button. Jessa's face appears on the monitor.

"Look, Terra, I know you've left for the Burn. I've known for a while you weren't happy here."

She sits in our room. She manually locked the door, not just relying on the computer locks that can be overridden. She brushes tears off her cheeks.

"I just wish you would have told me so that I could understand. I want to understand. Listen, I haven't told Dad yet that I know, but he's trying to sort through all the archives right now to figure out where you've gone. So wherever you are, please hurry and be safe. So you can get where you want to go without any of us stopping you."

There's a knock at the door. Jessa's head whips around. "Just wait a minute, Dad!"

"I've got to go. I think Dad's almost caught up. Listen, I love you. I know you were trying to tell me that all day yesterday. Be safe." Her face freezes on that moment, and my eyes burn. The screen goes black except for one line: Print text of message?

My finger hovers over the keys. Can I keep one reminder of her? One that I can actually touch? I too am crying. Then I press *Yes*.

The paper prints slowly. I find a waterproof cover and carefully slide the sheet in place, then fold it and lay it perfectly parallel to the edge of the bunk.

Needing something to cling to, my hands grab the folds of my dress. I look down. I need to change into the clothes Gaea gave me. The fabric is rough and dull colored, like brush-cleaning water. How often in painting class, one of the regular enrichment curriculums, we would paint a landscape. That is what the old masters painted. But the teachers never gave us a photo to paint from. Always the images in our heads. We weren't to be misled by what the Burn looked like before the Event. It would undoubtedly be a bastion of death and decay now, and those images were too violent, too corrupting to be allowed into the curriculum.

Now I will see it all. And it will be more magnificent than the images on Gaea's monitors. If it can look as beautiful as it did sent from a satellite to an outdated monitor several miles under the ocean's bulk, it will be astonishing in real life. It has to be.

I strip out of the dress. The Burn clothes are too big, but they'll do. I pull on the hiking boots, and my feet feel a hundred pounds heavier. All the shoes in the colony are feather light and small. These are clunky, but maybe you need something like this for walking on rocks.

I toss the dress in the bottom of the pack, put the clothes and other supplies on top, then fold Jessa's message twice more and slip it into a zippered pouch on the front.

I'm hungry finally, after the memory of swallowing blood has faded, so I search the sub's supply bins. A few energy bars, and a first-aid kit with a sedative. Just what I need to sleep until Washington.

When I wake up, my head feels heavy like a bucket of water. I don't feel rested, and my stomach cramps from eating too many energy bars. When the computer says, "Three miles to the New America coast," I vomit into the empty supply bin.

I gargle some water and wipe my mouth clean and force myself to breathe deeply. Then I notice the water through the window. It's still murky, but less oppressive and more open, and I feel like the floating metal tank I sit in is weightless in that half-light. The depth gauge reads 200 feet. I have never been this close to the surface before. The euphoria shrieks through my veins. I've seen this much light—just a shadow, really—and I ache to go higher.

I pull my trembling fingers from the controls. I need to follow the plan. I sit on my hands and lean back in the seat, watching the computer take us just high enough to skim along the ocean floor. The vague outline of the sloping ground, almost the same color as the water with the sand churning in the currents, hovers in front of the window. Is it stormy up there? The monitors show a pattern of swirling clouds and heavy rain. I don't have a poncho in the pack. After living for sixteen years in a metal shell, I didn't think about something like rain.

Is there any plastic sheeting in the sub? Sometimes the researchers use it to lay their specimens on. Yes, there in a cubby. It is a small sheet, maybe three feet square, but it's better than anything else at hand.

"One mile to the Puget Sound."

The sub slows even more, and the water turns brown. Bits of plant life roils through the currents. It must be really bad up there, and I have the first real, solid doubt I've had this whole trip. Can I weather even a storm? And if not a storm, how can I weather the people? I clutch my head and lean into the control panel, rocking myself to the sway of the sub as it buffets along through the turgid water.

The sub does its best to plow through, but it rocks back and forth, and I feel sick again. I lose track of time. But after what feels like hours later, the computer beeps at me, and we bank violently off course.

"Water patterns unstable. Suggest immediate docking."

Where? I check the topographical map. I'm well within the Puget Sound. There's Seattle, across the water, only five miles away. Gaea warned me about the cities. There's a jutting of land to the west; that will have to be as good as any other place to dock, and the stretch of water separates me from the city. With the way the sub lurches, I don't think I'll make it much farther as the land starts choking in on me and there's less room to navigate.

The bottom of the sub scrapes along the rocks, and I feel like they will pierce through the metal and scrape along the soles of my feet as well. But the sub shudders to a stop and sighs as the air locks around the hatch open.

The air outside hisses at me, and the rain beats a regular rhythm on every surface of the sub. I wrap the plastic sheeting around me best as I can and step outside. My shoes squeal on the wet rocks.

Then I hear shouting and a sound I've only heard one other time. A sound I heard when I watched the high-def footage of the Event. Gunfire. I duck to the ground. I don't know where the shots come from or if they're aimed at me. I look back to the sub. I want to crawl in and hide until the pops around me fade. But the sub already slips into the water, swimming for home.

I lie on the ground with my hands over my head, but the shouts and the gunfire don't stop. I look up, and the rain pours in my eyes. A hundred yards down the rocky beach, four figures waver in the rain. Three of them have long guns—rifles, I think—pointed out toward the water. The fourth rushes a boat into the water, jumps in, and starts the motor.

I lose some of the words against the rain and surf, but I hear bits of the shouting.

"Don't do it!"

"Are you crazy?"

"Cover me!"

On the water, a boat bobs farther out. Five or six men fire back at the people on the beach. They're too far away and all I can hear is the noise of their yells. Beyond them, I see faint wisps of light across the sound. Seattle. Is that where these men came from? Something tells me to be scared, to run. But my brain is numb and I'm paralyzed to the ground.

The small boat races out across the water. The man in it lies low as he steers, and the other three people on the beach aim at the larger boat.

"Stupid boy! Get out of the way! I don't want to blow your head off!"

The boat skips across the water, closer to the larger boat. The rain pelts down on him, but the man inside sits up and fires two shots at the boat. The first causes one of the men in the large boat to slump, and the others duck down. The second blows a hole in the boat close to the water. The men in the boat no longer care about the people on the shore. They scramble to where the water floods in.

The man in the small boat turns away quickly and aims for shore. But one of the men behind him stands up, aims his gun, and the motor explodes in smoke. The shot rocks the boat and the man inside falls into the water. His friends on shore can't see this—they think he's still in the boat. But I squint and he's floating in the water, held in place by the straps of his pack snagged on the boat. He tries to slip his arms out, but the wind whips the boat around and it bashes him on the head.

I'm racing toward the water and pulling my boots off before I even stop to think that I might not be able to swim in the roiling surf. The water shivers me from head to toe as soon as I dive

74

in. I pull arm over arm through the foamy water toward the boat. My first act on the Burn will be to save someone from drowning. What if this person wants to kill me afterward? What then? Ten minutes on the Burn and that will be the end. My arms ache with each stroke. I'm a proficient swimmer during daily exercises, but that's in a calm pool, not stormy waters. The shouts from shore fade into the waves.

Finally I reach the boat and haul myself into it. I slop into water, and I can hardly see through the rain streaming into my eyes. The boat is a third filled with ocean water from a gaping hole on one end. The man dangles from the boat, and his gun strap is tangled in his hands. I don't want to touch the gun. I don't want to be anywhere near it. I pull the strap from his hands, and the gun brushes my skin. It is cold as ice and jolts me to the shoulder. I drop it in the water.

Then I see the hook the man's pack is caught on, and I pull the knife from the sheath at my waist. I slice through a strap and he is free. Now I need to get him to shore. The boat sinks from under me, and we're both in the water. My legs churn feverishly, trying to keep us both afloat.

I thread his arms through the other strap so his pack is hitched up on his chest. His blond hair hangs in his face, and I can't see if he's conscious. He bobs for a moment then slips beneath the water. I dive after him, wrap my arms around his chest, and lay his head on my shoulder and kick toward shore.

The rain pelts my upturned face, stinging my eyes. I fasten my clenched fingers in the plaid shirt he wears and gasp as the coming waves slither over my face and into my nose. I choke and sputter, but still I kick. He moans up to the sky. He is alive. That knowledge buoys me almost to floating above the water. I kick until my lungs pound like feet stomping on my chest. I kick until I feel the gravely brush of shore beneath my heels.

I grab him under the armpits and drag him out of the water. I turn him on his side and thump his back, pounding the water out of him. The water gushes out of him less and less as I continue to hit him, until finally he coughs and retches into the rocks, and then breathes deeply. I turn him onto his back and brush the hair away from his face.

But is he ever beautiful. His skin is tanned golden brown, and his chapped lips are rough along the center of the bottom lip. His eyes are still closed, which worries me, but he is alive. His heavy, blonde eyebrows furrow, leaving two deep vertical lines between them.

I touch his cheeks rough with several days of unshaven beard. Past the stubble, sun-worn face, and sea salt crusted into his skin, I am surprised at how young he is—probably a couple years older than me. I touch his cheeks and hands. They're cold. I rub his hands. He moans again and moves his legs. He suddenly clenches my hand in his, and the touch burns my skin. His eyes flutter open, and then I hear voices on the beach. I take one last drink of him and he focuses on me briefly before closing his eyes again, and then I skitter behind a large sheet of scrap metal embedded in the rocks.

Three people make their way across the beach, two tall and one short, probably my height. They are phantom shadows through the drizzle of rain until they're about two hundred feet off, and then I can tell two are men and one is a woman. The woman and one of the men is about the same age as the young man I saved, and the other is older. The girl's brown hair escapes her poncho, running dark lines down her pale face. Her clothes are similar to mine. At least I won't look too out of place. Each of them carry a rifle.

"David!" The older man cups his hands around his mouth. The other two swivel their heads back and forth, combing the beach and the surf. They stop when they see him lying on the rocks.

"Dave!" The girl runs to him, flinging her gun to the ground. I flinch as it clanks among the rocks.

"Mary, don't throw that gun again. I've told you how dangerous it is." The older man bends down to pick up the rifle and stands guard over them. He strokes his red and gray beard with one hand.

She kneels by Dave and raises his head to rest on her knees. "Jack?" she says with a tremor.

Jack kneels next to them and runs his hands over Dave's body, then listens to his heart and breathing. He sighs.

"He's still alive. He'll be fine. A little water-logged, but fine."

Mary closes her eyes, and two tears stream down her cheeks, but it could have been the rain. I sigh in relief. I want to go to him, to see for myself, but then she caresses his face. At her touch, his eyes open again.

"Mary?"

Her face beams.

"Did you save me?" His voice is incredulous. I smile at his doubt. He remembers me after all.

Mary ignores the question and gently places his pack under his head. She's embarrassed that she threw herself to him.

"Someone saved me. I remember. I was in the boat." He tries to sit up, but Jack pushes him down again.

"Easy there, Dave."

"No, someone saved me. I was in the boat and when the raiders blew up the engine I knocked my head. Must've passed out. But I remember someone dragging me to shore. She left me here."

"She?" Mary raises an eyebrow.

"Yeah, she," he says angrily. He props himself up on an elbow. "She was like you, but not." He looks across the beach. "She must be here somewhere."

Mary rolls her eyes. "Right, Dave, right. Mystery women jumping in the water to save strangers and then disappearing into thin air. Maybe she was an agent, too. Or maybe you knocked your head harder than you think."

He glares at her. Then he turns and stares at the piece of metal I hide behind, and I swear he can see me. His eyes bore into mine through the miniscule gap I watch them through. I gasp and whip my hand over my mouth. There is no way he can see me here. My chest burns.

He stares hard one second more, then looks to Mary, and his eyes finally focus on her. "You're probably right."

The older man offers Dave his hand. "You up for walking, boy?"

Dave grasps the hand and pulls himself up. "Well, Red, I'd better be. We should get out of this rain." His hands sink to his knees for a moment as he gathers himself. I want to tell him to lay down and rest, but I can't move.

"They gone?" Red says.

Dave nods, looking at the water. "There were five on that boat. Scouting, maybe."

"Government headhunters?"

"No, raiders."

78

"They won't tell anyone we're here?" Red asks, clasping Dave's arm and helping him lurch ahead.

"No. I shot one and the others went down with the boat."

Jack falls in line behind them. "We'll have to close up early tonight, just to be sure."

Dave nods.

Red looks across the water where the motor boat drifts further from shore.

"You think it's salvageable?" Jack says.

"Nah." Red pulls on his beard. "It was in sorry shape to begin with and even worse now. Come on, Jack, help David along. Let's get back to the settlement before it gets too dark."

Dave puts an arm around Jack's shoulders and the four follow the paved road between old houses. My feet twitch. Should I follow them? I can't call out to them. All they would hear is a gagged moaning on the rain-slicked wind. They'll be repulsed. But I can't watch them disappear forever behind the ruined houses.

I sling my pack on my back and rustle the plastic sheeting around my head. At least I won't get rain in my eyes. My shoes slap the ground as I run after them, and I duck behind debris to stay carefully out of sight.

EIGHT

A large paved area (I think this is what Mr. Klein called a parking lot) leads to a street. The concrete is cracked and some comes up in chunks. The four people pick their way along a path they seem to know from memory, barely pausing to catch their footing on the uneven ground. I'm much slower as I trudge along in my heavy boots. I don't need to worry about staying far enough away; I need to worry about just keeping up.

Houses, mostly small simple buildings, line the street. They feel warm to me. The brick, wood, and colors of them have texture and depth that the plastic and metal from the colony could never match. I try to imagine people living in them. Now they are husks, with sad broken-window eyes dripping rain like tears into the overgrown vegetation. New trees spring up close to the houses, and the grass is up to my waist. In another hundred years, this might be a forest with the houses crumbling to dust. It makes me sad. How many people are at the settlement that all these houses go to waste? It can't be very large. David, Mary, Red, Jack, and a few others might be all there are.

I slip behind a building. Dave's head has been half-turning the entire time, like he has an itch he needs to scratch, to see if someone is there. If he only knew it is his mysterious rescuer following behind. I go around the back of the building, hoping to follow them from off the road and more carefully out of sight. Huge vats with rusted metal arms and long, rectangular pools sprawl before me, filled with rain water and leaves. Some sort of water treatment plant. We have filters and processors like this down in the colony, but much smaller. How inefficient these big ones must be. I remind myself that these are more than a hundred years old.

I pass a long double row of pools and reach a jumble of trees that hide me from the road. I peer through branches. The road ends maybe a thousand feet ahead of me, and Jack and Red's hunched forms waver in the distance as they help Dave turn the corner onto another street. I ignore the voice in my head telling me to be more discreet and I race ahead, following the marshy land to the west of me. It curves toward the street they follow, and there is plenty of brush to cover me.

Whatever their destination, they follow the decaying roads. I don't blame them. The roads cut swathes through weeds, new trees, and other debris. I thought following them off the road would be easier, but I change my mind as they more often fall out of sight and I stumble over dead, fallen trees and land up to my wrists in mud.

Weird, prickly balls from some of the plants stick to my pants and socks and the harder I try to rip them out of the fabric, the more of them cling to me. I yowl in frustration, and I sound like some caged animal. I plunge through the brush.

What am I doing following them? Dave has no idea who I am and I will never be able to tell him. He'll be repulsed—they all will be—and I'll wander out here on the Burn for the rest of my life because my tongue is cut out and I'm from the colonies, and people up here hate the colonies. How could I be so naive to think this would have worked?

The clouds are clearing and the sun hangs fat and red along the horizon. A large brick building hunkers up from the road south of me. A narrow strip of trees and rocks separate it from the Puget Sound. With Mary in the lead, the four figures climb steps that lead to a door. This must be the settlement. A sign next to the road says Junior High School. It is so different from our curriculum corridors in the colony. Everything there is so sterile. With the windows radiating light and the gentle murmur of voices, this building pulses with life.

I ignore my previous instincts to hide. I am here to meet these people, to become one of them. Scurrying through the trees out of sight is no way to do that. I can at least go and peek in a window. If they see me now, they see me.

I slide around the corner of the building and find a low window. Long tables line up and down the room, and about fifty people sit at them—more people than I thought there'd be. A short row of stainless steel carts with glass shields in front hold steaming piles of food. Two people dish up food onto old, chipped plates. There is a blue floral pattern on one, another is square and white. Another is cream and rimmed in silver. How odd that they don't match. I think of Jessa. She'd probably like how eccentric it all is.

82

Most of the people are about thirty or forty, though there are some younger like me and older like my grandma. A couple kids run around the tables, playing some dizzying game that I can't make out the rules to. Then my stomach falls.

There are watchers in every corner of the ceiling. But no, the lenses are smashed. A monitor that could be the great-grandfather to the one in my quarters hangs blank on the wall.

Three of the survivors hunch around a small metal box with knobs and an antennae. *Radio*, my Burn history lessons fill in for me. Their brows knot and they listen intently. One of them jots down notes every so often. Then one of them puts a hand to her mouth and they look at each other. They wave others over. Most of them stand around the radio when Dave and his group walk in.

They come through a swinging door on the left side of the room and an older woman stands up to greet them. She kisses Red, and he hugs her tightly. His eyes crinkle along the corners when he burrows his cheek in her silver hair.

I turn around and lean against the wall, sliding down until I sit on the ground. I'm an intruder watching the intimate homecoming. I take my pack off and wrap my arms around myself. I can't stay. They're a family, and I'm not one of them. I look west. The sun sets and lavender dark creeps around the school.

If I leave now, I'll probably stumble into something and kill myself. I'll stay until first light. I dig the blanket out of the pack and unfold it over myself. I contemplate an energy bar, but without my tongue I can't taste very well, and the memory of vomiting the others up turns my stomach. My lips are tight with thirst. I should go find water for my purifier, but I don't want to leave the faint comfort being near the settlement gives me.

I jump at a sound at the window. Curtains snap closed. I look around. Almost all the windows on the second floor are boarded up. All the windows on the ground floor are being shuttered or curtained. A muffled voice says, "The windows all dark?"

"Yeah, no light tonight."

My sleepy mind spins. Why can't they let any light out? I feel cold without the light shining on me. I pull the blanket up to my chin. When I close my eyes, all I hear is the pop of gunfire. I see a man slump over the side of a boat. But the images are far away, behind the haze of rain. I lay my head on the pack and fall asleep.

In my dreams I hear voices swirl on the wind around me.

"Who do you think she is?"

"She looks familiar to me."

"She can't have been wandering long. That or she knows what she's doing out here. She has some mild dehydration, but that's it."

"I don't recognize the pack. Looks military issue."

I feel them stiffen around me. A hand on my arm, turning it over.

"No tracker."

"She cut it out?"

"No tracker as in she's never had one."

A short breath. Then rough fingertips gently touch my face, brushing the hair from my eyes. "Yeah, she definitely looks familiar."

I crack open my eyes. It's raining again, and the water beads on the plastic sheeting and pours off on either side. I shiver.

84

"Look, guys, she's cold. I think we should bring her in."

Then I recognize Mary's voice. There's a hard edge to it. "We have no idea who she is." She pulls Dave from his crouch next to me and turns him to face her. "She could be anybody. She could be harmless, or she could be one of *them*."

Jack kneels down next to me. He runs his fingers along the blanket and eyes my pack. "This isn't stuff scrounged up from some abandoned house. Military or something. We'd better be careful." A vague fear creeps into his eyes.

"See?" Mary says.

Dave touches her arm. "Then we'll be careful." He squats down next to me again and shakes my shoulder. "Hey, wake up."

I finally flutter my eyes open, brushing out the rain that persistently falls on my face.

"Can you get up?"

My neck has a nasty crink and my back is stiff, but I'm alright. I fight the stiffness and stand, folding my blanket that somehow gave me away.

Dave crosses his arms and looks at me. Mary approves of the stance and adopts it herself, but she misses the compassion that gleams in his eyes.

"So who are you?"

My toes squirm in the heavy boots. The moment I've dreaded—a question requiring more than a nod or shake of the head. I can't just shrug my shoulders. I know who I am, and I can't lie to them about everything. I debate for another agonizing minute, when Mary steps forward and prods my shoulder with the barrel of a rifle.

"Come on, answer the question."

I see the suspicion like needles in her eyes. I hate her completely at that moment, and so I open my mutilated mouth wide for her, hoping it will disgust her into silence.

She whips a hand over her mouth. Jack whistles in a quick gasp. Only Dave stands unmoved, but I can't read anything on his face. I want to ask him if I can at least come in and eat something and warm up. But I don't look at him again. His face is too carefully guarded, and I can't tell if he's repulsed or concerned, and not knowing is too dangerous.

"You military?" he says. "And don't dare lie."

I shake my head.

"From a gang?"

I shake my head. At this rate he'll never guess who I am.

Finally he shakes the rain off the brim of his cap and walks to me with his right hand extended.

"I'm Dave."

His hand is warm and rough and he seems like the only stable fixture on the earth at this moment. I grab his hand with my other one as well. Mary makes a move forward, but Jack puts an arm out. She wrenches away.

I open Dave's hand and spell my name on his palm with my finger.

"Terra?" A smile breaks through the shield over his face. The smile warms me. I nod.

"Come on in. We can talk more about this inside."

Mary glares but doesn't try to stop me.

I look around for my pack and then notice it on Jack's shoulders.

"Oh, your pack?" Dave says. I nod. "Jack'll take it for you. Don't worry."

86

But I do worry. Printing off the message from Jessa was the stupidest thing I could have done. Even if the supplies don't give me away, the note certainly will. I need to get it back, but from my position now, I'm helpless.

I hobble along beside Dave. My legs are still half asleep from spending all night on the ground. Inside the school is a small lobby with restrooms off to one side.

"Do you need to use the bathroom?" Dave says.

I didn't notice outside. But now that my heart isn't racing, my bladder catches up with me. I nod emphatically. Jack laughs and points to the door marked with the silhouette of a girl.

The facilities are crude, but the toilet flushes and water runs into the sink. I didn't think about things like running water when I made my way through the Pacific Ocean. Is this a luxury?

When I come back out, Jack and Mary are both gone. I cock an eyebrow at Dave to ask the question. He smiles.

"They went into the cafeteria to breakfast."

I shake my head. Wrong question. Don't get frustrated, I remind myself. This will take some practice for both of us.

"What then?"

I try to make the sound of rushing water. It sounds more like a cat hocking up a fur ball. I growl. Then I make the motion of washing my hands.

"The running water?"

I nod, happy to not have to resort to making more savage noises again.

"That's one of the first things we got working when we decided on the school for the settlement. It took some time, but it really wasn't that hard. Turns out everyone was pretty willing to put some elbow grease in when faced with the thought of digging a latrine out back." He chuckles at the memory, and I love the sound. I smile with him, careful to keep my teeth closed. He scratches his cheek.

"You really look familiar to me. Have you been up to Washington before?"

Before I can even think through an answer, I shake my head. I can't lie to him. His eyes are too earnest.

"Yeah, you're probably from down south, judging from the way your skin is peeling." He touches my cheek with a rough fingertip and I shiver. I hope he doesn't notice.

"Still cold?" Worry laces his voice. Understandably. With the sun coming up, everything is warming and drying off. I can't hide anything from him.

I shake my head and put a hand to my stomach.

"Hungry?"

I nod.

"That's my girl," he says, indicating the doors to the cafeteria. How easy it is to fall in step alongside him. He's about a foot taller than I am, and I feel comfortable walking next to him, like his shadow would. I'm safe there, even from Mary's frosty stare as we walk into the cafeteria.

Dave steers me to the food carts, and an older man with shining, red cheeks ladles me up some gloopy oatmeal.

"Strawberries, too?" he says.

I pause. I have a choice? I founder for a moment, lost in the limbo of indecision. I've always had my food prescribed. I always had to eat every bit—it was optimized of course, down to the last teaspoon. But now, I have a choice. I won't be able to taste the strawberries, but they look delicious.

I nod.

He scoops a generous portion of sliced strawberries on top of my cereal. Then he winks.

"And we even have a little honey this morning, so they're sweetened, too."

The first time I'll be able to try something unnecessarily sweetened, and I won't be able to taste much of anything. But this is my sacrifice. This is what I gave up to be on the Burn. I harden myself just a bit. I've hardened just about every part of me to deal with the colonies. I can handle not tasting food. Small sacrifices, I tell myself. I take the tray he offers me.

As we walk to a table, I notice the radio. Two people listen, but all I hear is static. One flips through a notebook while they eat breakfast. Jack waves us to the table where he and Mary sit. Mary shoots me daggers the whole time, but pats the bench next to her for Dave. Dave smiles, then side-steps and leads me to where Red eats with his silver-haired companion.

"Red, Nell, this is Terra."

I bob my head to them. Nell's mouth widens into an irresistible smile full of white, crooked teeth. I smile wide back, opening my teeth in spite of myself. But Nell doesn't flinch. She extends a soft, wrinkled hand. I shake it gently, almost an apology for showing my mouth to her.

"Not to worry, dear. You'll find all of us have our own scars here. Not everyone's is as obvious, but we're all just a bit broken. Comes with the territory."

I spoon some oatmeal and strawberries and put them in my mouth. I faintly taste a trace of the sweet. It isn't much, but it's enough. Dave smiles as I down three more bites. After the energy bars in the sub, this food, tasteless or not, is heavenly.

Red looks like he wants to ask more about my mouth, but Nell lays a hand on his arm. Red puts an arm around her shoulders and squeezes her. She smiles.

I peer out the window behind them. A realization strikes me in the chest. Through the window, I see the sky blue and hazy in the morning sunlight. Trees sway. I can see out the window and really *see*. No black ocean, no heavy weight. I walked through the rain last night and slept in it. I woke up to rain on my face this morning. And here I am looking through the window at a world illuminated by sunlight.

"What's wrong?" Dave says.

"Hmm?"

"You're crying."

I realize my face is wet. I sit here with two people who have spent their lives together on the Burn and are so completely in love, I can feel the emotion radiating off them. In the colonies we are led to believe that such a thing is impossible—the Burn is filled with killers and destroyers and such things as love and hope are shadows.

I shrug. I don't have the ability to tell him how happy I am at this moment.

NINE

After breakfast, Dave takes me on a tour of the settlement. Mary and Jack offer to accompany us, but Dave gives Jack a meaningful look and he quickly ushers Mary away. I raise an eyebrow.

"What was that all about?" he asks. I nod.

"Oh, just Mary being Mary. I love her, I do, but." He runs his hand through his hair, his lips stumbling as he feels for the right words. He and Mary must have some kind of past together and the current situation isn't comfortable for either of them. I wait.

"I can't do it right now. She's wanted to get back together ever since she came back from Seattle two months ago, but I'm not ready. She's changed since she came back."

He leads me up a flight of stairs. The stairs are patched in places, but I'm amazed how intact everything is. I was expecting total devastation. The floors need a good mopping and waxing, but everything is decent.

"Everybody sleeps up here. Some people share rooms, others have smaller rooms for their own. The town was evacuated when sirens announced a bombing. Most people thought Seattle would be safe—smaller city, nothing to protect. I guess they were right, it wasn't leveled. But it's dangerous. That's where Mary went a year and a half ago. Said she needed something different, thought she'd like it better. Dreams of building it up, changing it. You can guess how that went."

He pulls aside the thick fabric covering a window. Above the trees the gray water of the sound ripples out. In the distance across the water, I see the faint, irregular outline of ragged buildings.

"Seattle," Dave says. "There's an important rule we have. I don't know who you are really, but you can help me figure that out by how well you follow the rules."

I nod. I can follow rules. I grew up surrounded by them.

"The windows are covered before dusk. No light ever escapes them." His voice drops and his face is deadly serious. "Seattle can't ever know we're here."

He scares me. How bad can Seattle be? He meticulously puts the fabric back.

"The country's the place to be these days. Nothing to loot, nothing to claim. Gangs leave it alone, as long as they don't think there's anything here. The government leaves it alone as long as they don't know we're here. But you probably know that, it must be similar down south."

This time I'm ready for questions. I nod and try to appear understanding, though the only thing I understand is about the city. Gaea told me it was illegal to live outside one. Gaea also mentioned Arizona when we discussed where I should go. I'm from Arizona. It's inhospitable, surely I would want to leave it for somewhere greener. That isn't too far from the truth, really. I can feed him lies veiled in half-truths.

He motions to a door. "Here we are. This is where I live."

The room is the size of a classroom down in the colony. I half-expected to see it full of desks, but most of them are gone. Two desks remain, used for tables and storage space. A watcher haunts a corner of the ceiling, but just like in the cafeteria, its lens is destroyed. I remember what Gaea said about privacy invasions to prevent terrorism. Were the watchers part of that? Did the survivors rebel before or after the Event?

"Want to come in?"

I nod. A mattress lays on the floor, covered with a well-patched blanket. A candle is propped in a cup on one of the desks next to the bed. A few yellowed books are stacked on the floor. A small window is flung open to let the breeze waft through the room and clear the summer stuffiness. I breathe deeply. The air smells warm and grassy.

"It's like you're experiencing everything for the first time. The rain when we found you this morning, the oatmeal, and now this."

He sits on the bed. "I wish I could talk with you easier." He clears his throat. His gaze is so intense I turn away. I notice an old dog-eared, torn copy of *Jane Eyre*. I have never held a book in my hands; all of our texts are digital. Mr. Klein has some of the only physical books in the colony. I carefully run my fingers over the cover.

"I smuggled those here. My dad found them in an illegal library. After that ridiculous book ban ten years before the Event—"

They called it the Event, too.

"Everyone tried to snatch up books before they were all burned. Isn't it crazy? Stop people reading to try to stop them getting violent ideas. Sometimes I think it was finally about time they blew each other up." Then he clears his throat again and drops his eyes. Can he get in trouble for saying such things? I reverently place the book on top of the stack.

"I need to know where you're from and why you're here."

I sit down on the corner of his bed, carefully as far away from him on there as I can be. This delicate moment could ruin me. I'm not ready to let it go now. I motion for a piece of paper and a writing utensil. He scrounges around for a few minutes.

"We only use these to record what we hear on the radio. We try to use these sparingly, but I think now is a good time."

He hands me a yellowed piece of paper and a stubby pencil, and I put the paper on the desk and write.

"Arizona? You're a long way from home. Well, that explains the sunburn."

I nod.

"But why'd you leave?"

I write again.

"The desert?" He laughs. "Yeah, I bet. You came to the right place then."

I smile along with him. This is easier than I thought.

"Did you come by yourself? Does anyone else know you're here?"

There it is again—that seriousness. The fierce protection of the settlement, but from what? I remember the men Dave killed yesterday.

94

I'm not sure how to answer. Is it believable for a girl like me to travel alone? Did people do that here? The citizens are required to live in cities. I come from the outside. Dave lives on the outside. But could I have traveled this whole way without getting caught? The pencil hovers over the paper. Dave sits expectantly, his face neutral, not betraying a good answer. I scribble furiously, and my stomach drops with the lies I weave.

"Your mom died, so you decided it was time to leave? There were a couple others moving on too, so you traveled with them to northern California, then left them to come up here?"

I hope it's believable. His eyebrows furrow. I want to use one of my fingers to smooth out the furrows, to assure him I'm not a threat, but I clutch the pencil tightly. I still need to learn where I fit in here.

"But why come all the way up here by yourself? It's so dangerous traveling alone."

My heart pounds as this story races further away from me, almost out of my control.

A fresh start. I just needed to get away. I felt suffocated. I almost got caught, but I slipped away.

He studies me for a long moment; then his posture relaxes and he leans back on his hands.

"I can relate to that."

My shoulders slump in relief.

So who are you?

"I guess that's a fair question." He runs his fingers through his hair. "My dad was the unspoken leader of this settlement. When he died a year and a half ago, that just kinda passed on to me, unfortunately."

He does have the natural bearing of a leader, and people obviously look up to him, but he's so young. I remember my dad telling me I should try public office as a vocation. I can completely relate to the being-somewhere-you-don't-want-to-be thing.

"One of these days I'll ask you what happened to your mouth, but we'll save it for later. Do you want to stay here with us? Is this far away enough from whatever you were running from?"

I almost jump off the bed in exaltation. I pump my head up and down, not even trying to hide my smile.

He laughs. I don't care that he's laughing at me. He just gave me what I've needed for so many years.

"I guess that's settled. We'll figure out where you can stay in a little bit. In the meantime, there's your pack."

My pack. I forgot. I whirl to it and carefully open the flap to make sure everything is in place.

"Don't worry. I had Jack bring it straight up here. No one touched your stuff. You'll have to learn to trust people more here. Don't trust outsiders. Listen to me, I'm a hypocrite. I honestly don't know why I trust you. We're wired not to. That's why Mary is the way she is. But here, we're family. And if people think you don't trust them, they'll get upset."

I can trust them. But I'm sad because they shouldn't trust me. I'm nothing but lies. But I will do my best to be everything else to them I can. Whatever work they do, whatever help they need is all I can do to repay them.

"Now let's go. There's work to be done."

Back downstairs, fifteen of the group put on wide brim hats and grab hoes and rakes from a closet just inside the huge double doors that lead outside. They laugh and chat, and Dave falls in among them. I hang behind.

"They're going to check the crops. I'm actually on farming duty today too. Want to come?"

I laugh. Agriculture of all things. I may not have enjoyed it in the colony, but it's a job I'm half capable of. The tools are more rustic than what I'm used to, but I'll manage.

"Sorry about the primitive stuff. We didn't want to sign up for fuel rations for farm equipment. One more way for the government to take notice."

I shrug. The equipment's not a big deal, but I don't think I should ask about the rest of it yet. He talks about the government like I should know exactly what's going on.

Dave grabs me a hat from the closet and plops it on my head. It falls over my eyes. "Perfect fit. Let's go."

I fall in step beside him and we walk into the sunlight. The rain clouds clear to faint wisps in the distance. Despite the heat, everyone wears longs sleeves and pants. It reminds me of the radiation suits. But they aren't confined to sight behind visors, and they aren't temperature regulated. A single drop of sweat trickles down the valley my spine makes in my back. It's real. Everything here is real.

"Ran out of our government ration of sunblock a month ago," Dave says. "We're hoping for another supply drop soon, or we're all going to be crispy. Jack says we're low on meds as well."

Now it is too real. They only get medicine when the government rations it out?

We walk a few hundred yards to a huge patch of green plants with small, heart shaped leaves. The first of the workers are already moving up and down the messy, irregular rows, plucking plants from the ground. Why aren't the rows neater? It would make tending the field easier.

"We're weeding today." Dave takes his canteen off his shoulder and sets it next to an empty row.

I've never picked weeds before. We don't have them in the colony—there aren't random seeds in the air or sown in the fields from years ago that could suddenly germinate. Weeds just don't happen there. I stare at the field.

"You're from the desert part of Arizona?"

I nod.

"You probably don't have a lot of farming experience, huh?"

I shake my head, mystified about what I'm supposed to do here.

"No worries. I'll show you."

He kneels down and shows me a plant different from the others.

"We're growing oca tubers. So anything that's different from this," he shows me a big handful of the foliage, "just pick it out. Carefully, so you don't disturb the roots. These tubers are one of our staples during the winter, so they're precious. Treat them that way."

I nod and kneel down. The mud squelches against my pants, and I feel the moisture on my skin. So much like the time I went onto Field #3 without my suit. I reach down and pull a weed out. In the moist soil, it comes free easily in a big clump of weed, roots, and dirt.

"A little more gently next time," Dave says. "We don't want to take all the dirt from the field."

I put the weed in the bag sitting between us. Dave is already several feet away from me, making his way through the row. I set to work.

The sun rises high overhead, and the sweat trickles from my hair and into my eyes. I wipe the sweat and rub dirt across my face. My hands ache. They're raw from pulling the rough weeds. I always wore gloves, and my hands are too soft for this work. I grit my teeth and bend to another weed, digging softly to loosen it from the ground without disturbing the tubers.

I sit up and look down the row. Dave is a hundred feet from me and shows no sign of stopping. I flex my fingers. Someone laughs.

"Hard work the first time, isn't it?"

Nell kneels down beside me. Her shirt sleeves are rolled once, so her wrists show. Her hat perches on her silver hair, and a faded purple ribbon blows about her face.

"I'm getting too old for this, but I do love gardening. Those hydrangeas by the school were my idea. I thought it brightened it up." She offers me her canteen, and I take a long drink of warm water.

"I had to fight for them, of course. Anything too cultivated looks suspicious from the air, and we do get fly-overs every few weeks."

That explains the irregular oca rows. Neat rows would be too conspicuous from the sky. But I still don't understand why exactly they're hiding. What would happen if the government found out they're here?

"I remember the first day Red and I came to the settlement. Forty-six years ago. We found each other near Seattle, both of us running from the city, or what was left of it. It wasn't so bad at first. The government used trackers to be sure everyone got equal rations." She shows me a white, wrinkled patch of skin on the underside of her forearm. "I cut it out the day I left. The trackers were becoming a way for them to know where every person was at every moment. When I found Red, he protected me, and we wandered together, hoping to find something better. We came here and have been here ever since. There were only five others here back then, and they hadn't yet settled down in the school."

I smile at the warmth of her memories. But I have a weight in my gut that's been building since I landed here. At first glance, the hazy summer morning is idyllic. But the way these people talk, they're hunted every minute of their lives.

Nell's eyes sparkle. "I see a lot of that in you — the wanting to find something better."

She bends down, and her knobby fingers gently lift a weed out. She puts it in the bag next to me.

"There's a lot of people here who want to find something better. Who don't like living scared. But with the way the world is, I don't think they will. I'd rather live scared than live across the sound with *them*."

I need to get back to work, to distract myself from the world Nell creates for me, a world that sounds like the colony spinning out of control. But she tsks when she sees my cramped hands.

"Don't push yourself too hard the first day, or you won't be able to help the second." She pulls my hands free of the dirt.

100

"Why don't you just sit here and rest for a minute while I do the weeding? I could use the conversation. Red's knees are too arthritic for all this kneeling. He works in the kitchen mostly. Dave tells me you're from the Arizona desert, so you're probably not much used to our kind of farming."

I shake my head, wincing as I rub my sore fingers.

"That's alright. There's probably things you might be able to teach us. Old dogs, you know." And she winks at me. I can't help but giggle. She's as old as my grandmother, but nothing like her. Nell instantly puts me at ease.

"Dave told me a few details of your conversation this morning."

I raise an eyebrow. How quickly does news travel here? She smiles.

"You're right, in a place like this, I'm surprised he didn't just shout it in the cafeteria. Dave is a special one, and I think he's fond of you, right quick."

She crawls along a few feet to an unweeded patch. I carry the weed bag for her. I itch for her to continue her train of thought, but I don't want to rush her. She's the type of person who shouldn't be rushed.

The sun is just overhead, and two figures come from the school. The shorter one carries a big tray, and the taller one carries a jug.

"That'll be Jack and Mary with the lunch," Nell says. "Let's go eat."

Lunch is simple: bread, strawberries, sharp cheese, and water. It's strawberry season, and while our group weeds the tuber field, another group has been picking the strawberries before they get too ripe. Nell tells me, "If you don't get the strawberries, the birds will."

Nell explains that one of the biggest challenges is keeping the wildlife out of the fields. Someone always patrols the fields, day and night, to keep the animals away. Red enjoys the job, it doesn't bother his arthritis, and he likes to carry a gun. I laugh.

"What's so funny?" Dave brings over his lunch and sits down beside us. I'm unable to stop laughing. I point to Nell.

"Just telling Terra that Red is a little gun happy." She takes a dainty nibble of her cheese.

Dave nods. "But at least he's safe about it. Better than some people." He nods toward Mary. She glances over her shoulder at us. Her rifle lays slung across her back. I remember the disgust on Red's face when she threw the gun on the beach. "She always has that thing with her, even when she's here in the middle of us."

Nell studies him. "She's been through a lot, over in Seattle. A lot I can relate to. Did you ever ask her about it?"

Dave shifts side-to-side. "Well, no. You know how awkward it's been ever since she's been back."

Nell nods. "The only thing I'll say is you have no one to blame but yourselves. Now I'll let it rest. But Terra's good company." Then she walks away to sit down by another small cluster of workers.

The blush creeps up my cheeks, and I hope that out here in the sun and heat, Dave can't see it.

"Sometimes I think she's just a meddling busy-body." He bites a huge chunk of bread. I scowl at him for the less-than-stellar appraisal of Nell—she's quickly becoming a very good friend. He laughs, half-choking on the bread as he swallows.

102

"I guess good ol' Nell has you under her spell already. Funny how she can do that to people. I still haven't figured it out yet." He rubs a hand on the back of his neck. His perplexed look makes me laugh. He bumps my shoulder with his own.

"And I love how easily you laugh. I think that's your spell."

I'm about to grasp his hand, to spell something there, but a series of three sharp whoops cuts through the air, and the playful look on Dave's face vanishes. All around me, people scrabble for their tools and dash toward the trees.

TEN

Dave clutches my hand and yanks me to my feet.

"Hurry! Gather your things—get everything. There's choppers coming."

I frantically grasp at my plate and cup. The strawberries slide to the ground. I look around once more. There's nothing else. Dave already has the weed bag. He grabs my elbow and almost wrenches my arm off as he breaks into a run and pulls me along. We jump over the rows of oca. His legs stretch into long strides, and I can hardly lift my boots that high and my feet slog around in them, throwing off my balance. I stumble and fall in a cushion of plants. My first thought is that I destroyed someone's meal this winter. But Dave's ashen face tells me this shouldn't be my first concern. Ahead of us, Nell hurries, but can't move fast enough.

"Go, Terra!" Dave yells.

From the direction of the water, I hear a noise that splits the air and thuds against my ears. I untangle myself and look back.

There is nothing but blue sky. The picture is so serene, but I feel the terror pressing against my chest. I can't breathe—the air only comes in gasps.

Dave scoops up Nell in his arms. He barrels through the remaining oca. Nell clings to him like a frightened child. She is small and frail as one. Her face is white.

I race across the wide sweep of long grass, following the trails the others made as they sprinted for cover. I remember the stories Mr. Klein told us about hunts in England. Foxes being chased by huge hounds and men and women on horseback. I feel like that fox, now, with nothing but my legs to keep myself from danger. I am exposed here in the grass; anything could catch me here. But I'm still not sure what I run from.

I duck behind a tree and peer around. Dave staggers. His face is red and his forehead pulses. But he won't let go of Nell, even as he starts to fall into the shadow of trees. Another man jumps out and catches Nell just as they reach us. Dave crouches on the ground next to me, his breath coming in ragged gasps.

The canopy of leaves reaches its shadow out and then the sun slices it and everything else glows. In the distance, two black birds fly toward us. But they aren't birds. They have propellers and they don't swoop in the sky. They trace a course straight toward the school. Nell trembles and squeezes my hand.

"Don't move," Dave says.

We all collectively hold our breaths. The helicopters are close enough now that I see huge machine guns mounted to the sides. Nell told me there were flyovers. I hadn't dreamed the helicopters would look like angels of death.

They hang suspended over the school for several seconds. Then they sweep toward us and over the oca field. The oca billows under the beating air. I've been crouching too long and my legs cramp up. I want to scream. But one look at Nell's face steadies me. Her lips tremble, but her eyes shine with defiance.

"What are they looking at?" Dave looks back into a dozen wide eyes. "Did anyone leave anything behind?"

We all shake our heads in unison. And then a gasp and a woman points. On the field is an abandoned weed bag.

"They won't see it," Dave says. "It's the same color as the dirt. They won't see it."

He's trying to convince himself. I want to believe him, but the helicopters hover for an eternity. I can see the open door. A gleam of glass from the door, and then a pinprick of light. I hiss and grab Dave's hand.

Have they ever taken pictures before?

He shakes his head numbly, like he doesn't even realize what I asked him. His face sags.

The helicopters hover over the field for another moment, then tilt toward the west and are gone. I still hear the chop drumming in my ears.

After an hour, we finally move.

"We're done for the day. No more work. Back to the school." Dave is no longer pale, but his face is craggy.

The silence is as tangible as sand on my skin as we break from our crouches. No one wants to be the first out from under the trees. Nell slips her hand into Dave's and lets him lead her toward the oca field. The rest of us fall in line.

"And someone get that bag," Dave says.

The sun is orange and heavy and I stumble, my legs numb with kneeling and the hiking boots. Now that we are out of the shadow, Dave flicks me a smile.

"You'd better get your energy back. You came on just the right day—we're having a bonfire to celebrate the strawberry harvest."

A celebration? Now?

"Maybe you didn't have bonfires in Arizona with how dry and hot it is. Well, we build a great big fire and we dance and sing and talk."

I can't believe he's talking about having a party after this afternoon. I don't know what would have happened if those helicopters had found exactly what they were looking for, but I don't need to. I saw the terror in everyone's faces and felt the stone in my own stomach and knew it would be disaster for everyone. And now Dave says they're going to dance?

"I know. It seems wrong somehow. But I think it'll be better this way. Everyone won't brood on it too long."

I just escaped one world with dances that I dreaded, just to come to another dance. I glare. That brightens Dave's face.

"Oh, come on! It won't be that bad, I promise. And if it is, I'll show you where you can hide out and avoid the whole thing."

I glance sidelong at him. He rolls his eyes.

"You're coming to at least try it out. I'll stay right by you." Then he leans down conspiratorially. "I won't let Mary and her rifle anywhere near you."

I guffaw so loud that several people turn to look at me, and I slap a hand over my mouth.

107

As we come in the school, several people disappear up the stairs. Red stands in the lobby waiting. He sees Nell and hugs her against his chest.

"She's fine, Red. I helped her to the trees."

Red reaches out a hand and shakes Dave's fervently. "They find anything?"

"They took pictures this time."

Red tightens his grip on Nell. "I don't know how much longer we can stay here. Those flyovers are coming more frequently."

Dave nods. "Like they're putting together the puzzle pieces."

Red kisses Nell's hair. "I'm sending everyone up to get the windows closed early. We're all a little on edge."

"We're still having the bonfire," Dave says.

Red half-smiles. "I figure you'd want to. Probably be good to distract everyone. Come on in to dinner."

I grab a plate of food. As I walk to a table, I see Jack sitting by the radio. His plate of food is on one knee, the pad of paper and pencil on another. His hazel eyes brighten and he waves me over. He's probably Dave's age, maybe two years older than me.

"Do you want to listen in?" he asks.

I nod. I hear the crackle and whisper of the radio every time I'm in the cafeteria. There is always someone listening, ready to write. I want to know what they listen to.

Jack hands me the notebook and pencil. "You can be record keeper."

I hold the pencil. What do I write?

"Did you have a radio in Arizona?"

I shake my head.

108

"How did you keep up with what was going on in the government?"

The government? Is the radio the only way they know what's going on?

I shrug. Jack shakes his head.

"No wonder everything's such a nightmare. There's still people who can't even hear them."

From what I've seen, that's not the problem. It's the methods they use to control the country.

"Alright then, just write down important things. I'll help you figure it out."

I bend over the notebook, and Jack chews his food. Every few minutes, the radio whines at us, but we hear nothing. I look at Jack.

"Sometimes it's like this, other times there's a lot going on."

Then an echoey voice comes out.

"The uprisings in Portland ended peacefully this morning. Forty-five citizens were detained for questioning. The rest were dismissed to their homes. We remind citizens of every city that the cities exist for your protection. In the wilderness, we cannot protect you from dangers both internal and from foreign nations. Anyone found outside city limits will be detained for questioning."

Jack laughs grimly. "That's a euphemism for put in a labor camp. I swear they have to open a new one every day for how many people have been 'detained for questioning.' Write down that the uprising in Portland is over."

I scribble furiously. Then the radio lies quiet for several minutes. I take a bite of food. Jack eats his, but he doesn't say anything more. His eyes are thoughtful. Then the radio crackles again.

"Updated supply-drop schedule."

Jack's head whips up, and he taps the paper. This is important.

"All drops will take place in two days at nine o'clock in the morning. The following cities in western New America will receive food drops: Portland, Sacramento, and Phoenix. The following cities in western New America will receive medical drops: Seattle, Salt Lake City, and San Diego. No other drops are scheduled at this time."

Jack waves Dave over.

"Med drop in two days," Jack says.

Dave nods. "Well, that explains the fly over today. They usually scout around a bit when there's a drop scheduled. I'll talk to Red about it tonight."

After dinner, everyone heads out behind the school. Red and Jack have already started the fire under the thick boughs of a cluster of trees that I instinctively know shield us from watching eyes. I wrap my arms around my shoulders and shiver. It isn't cold, but watching the fire—a real fire—jump heavenward is breathtaking. Fires, candles, gas stoves, anything that burns, aren't allowed in the colonies. This fire warms the icy pit in my stomach, and the terror of the afternoon loosens. The others gathered here feel it as well. Their talk is freer, and they laugh. Watching the orange and yellow fingers writhe and dance, I feel the urge to dance too.

What's wrong with me? I hate dancing. I've been to a dance only once—four days ago—and solely as a means to get here. I refused Jessa's pleas every time, and she looked so disappointed. She just wanted me to come and have fun—it was hard to spend too much time together. My heart ached every time I told her no, but I insisted. I wouldn't be a fool like all the others, dancing to some ethereal, synthesized music like everyone else.

I think of Jessa dancing a few days ago, swaying with Brant to the music. The way they all swayed. There was no other way to dance to that music. How happy she was, thinking I was there, actually trying it out for once. And then I think how crushed she was when she realized I had left forever. I think of the message she left me. I try to force it from my mind. It's too painful and too dangerous to think of her, but I can't help it. She was devastated, but understanding. How could I do that to her?

Thinking about Jessa, my feet start moving without my realizing and I dance up to the fire, moving to no particular beat, my feet aching with every step in my too-heavy boots, raising my tired legs and stomping wildly. A voice laughs at me. Mary's, no doubt. But I don't care. I dance for Jessa. I dance because there is actually a reason to dance—I am alive, and so are these people, and now that the fear and thud of the helicopters are gone, I have had the best day of my life. I jump up and down, my lungs pumping, my heart racing with the life I feel flow through me. My dance isn't pretty, but I can't say how I feel—I need to show it.

I circle the fire with my crazy dance, and as I spin from the blaze, a long shadow joins mine, dancing not quite as wildly, but adding to my dance, complementing it. I look up. Dave is a few feet away from me.

"You look ridiculous, but I couldn't let you have all the fun."

I grin and speed up the whirlwind.

Then a voice sounds from somewhere among the circle of onlookers. A deep, rich voice using no particular words but sounding out a musical rhythm, frantic to keep up with the dancers. Someone has a pot and bangs it with a spoon to keep the beat.

Across the fire Nell and Red join the dance, but slower, more deliberate. They hold hands and step in time to the rhythm. All around the circle, more people stomp and sway and clap. But Mary stands stiffly, her rifle slung over her back, her arms folded.

I dance over to Nell and Red. I stand by them and watch the fire glow. Then I hear Mary's voice. She whispers to Jack, but she's so agitated I can hear every word.

"She's got to be military."

Jack raises an eyebrow. "Why?"

"Did you see those soft, white hands? She hasn't done a day of hard work in her life."

"It doesn't mean anything. There's probably too many people out there still living off the government rations. She's one of them. Came from Phoenix, probably; snuck rations all her life."

"No, she's too healthy. And no tracker, remember? A desk job. Maybe an agent. I'm telling you, because of her, they're going to find us. She's here one day and there's a fly over. Perfect timing, if you ask me. Because of her, they'll turn this settlement into a labor camp as fast as you can blink, and they won't stop to ask why only a few of us have trackers. We'll all be slaves in no time."

Jack shifts his weight, but says nothing. Then after a moment, he clears his throat.

"If Dave trusts her—"

Mary snorts.

I can't listen to this, listen to who they think I am. I can't do a thing to deny it. Nothing I say will convince Mary. I sit on a log next to Dave. The fire dies down, and as it slumps lower to the ground, the dancing ebbs and the singing turns to lullabies whispered to each other. I stare at the fire, at the shimmering coals. A log pops and a blizzard of sparks flies up into the sky to join the stars. My face is hot from sitting too close to the fire, but I don't want to scoot back.

Dave puts a hand on my arm. "You're loving this, aren't you?"

I start back. He could never guess what I've been thinking. How I miss Jessa so much I want to cry, how terrified I was of the helicopters earlier today, how I've never seen a fire burning. But I can't tell him that. Let him think what he wants to for now.

"I can tell. You show everything on your face, Terra. I like that."

I smile back at him and pat the hand on my arm. Should I do more than that? I don't want to with Mary's gaze on us, even if Dave doesn't seem to mind. She has watched us all evening. She's suspicious of me, and she has a prior claim. From what I learned from Dave and Nell, that much is sure. I can't risk upsetting that. This is a tightly woven group of people. If I do anything to unravel it, I won't be able to live with myself. But I feel so strongly about Dave. Not love, not that, I don't think. That should feel more like a tugging at my heart. I feel a warmth there, like a blossom. More than friends. What we have transcends friendship. I saved his life, and he gave me my dream. I will do just about anything for him.

Regardless of Mary's stare, I lean into him, just slightly. He squeezes my arm. He looks at me, and I see the uncertainty on his face. What he is uncertain about, though, I can only guess.

"There's something I want to tell you." He clears his throat and looks through the fire, and doesn't say anything more. I watch shadows flicker across his face.

"Something happened to me yesterday, and it really changed me."

My heart races ahead to where this could lead. The rescue. Does he know it was me?

"I was in a boat, testing it out. We need all the boats we can get for supply drops. The sound is dangerous, but not as dangerous as traveling on foot. Unfortunately, no one in the settlement knows how to build a boat, and we don't want to go advertising for wandering boat makers. I wanted to try it in the storm to see if it could really hold, but of course Jack and Mary thought that was a bad idea. Red didn't mind, though. He saw where I was going with the whole thing."

Where is he going with this conversation? It seems like he doesn't want to get to the point. I glance at him once, encouraging him to go on.

"The water probably was too rough; I should have listened to Jack. But I wanted to try anyway. I made it just past the point, and then the pirates came."

I raise my eyebrows.

"Raiders, pirates, whatever."

So that's who they were. Pirates. I read about them for Burn history. European Burn history. But real pirates?

Dave looks away from me. "They had already seen us, and we couldn't pick them off from shore. So I put the boat back in

114

the water. There was no way I could get away from them. The rain was pouring in my face and there was already too much water in the boat. We got rid of them, but I crashed the boat and totally clobbered my head. I think I was tossed from the boat—I was so out of it I can't be sure."

He runs a hand through his hair, and rubs his knees. He doesn't realize he's telling me what I already know. I saw it all. I can give him a more accurate version.

"When I woke up, all I saw was the most beautiful face with dark hair looking over me. Only for a second, and then she was gone, and now I'm not even sure she was there. I was so out of it. I love that face. Not *in* love, I don't think. But I love her. Does that make any sense? She looked at me like I was the first and last person she ever wanted to see. And her eyes—there was so much depth to them. Like your eyes. I can't describe it. Then I heard Mary's voice. Red, Jack, and Mary said they didn't see anyone. She must have gone too fast."

He turns to me, scrutinizing every angle of my face.

"It could have been Mary, I guess. That face, I don't know. She looked a lot like you." He tucks a strand of hair behind my ear and laughs. If only he knew. I ache to tell him. He doesn't know it's me he loves. He feels the same way I do—we love each other. Not *in* love. That is a good way to describe it. We aren't there yet.

Then my shoulders sink. I can't tell him. I told him my story, and it didn't include rescuing him. To change that now will raise too many questions. Dave shifts uncomfortably next to me.

"I don't know if I'll ever find her. If she hasn't found our settlement by now, I don't think she meant to stay around. It could just be Mary."

Is he trying to convince himself?

He laughs again. "I could just be going crazy." He touches my chin with his fingers, raising my head up to meet his eyes.

"But you remind me of her. And there's so much honesty in your face. I don't think I could let you go. Not after losing her, too. Will you stay here with us, for a while at least?"

I smile, sadly I know, but smile. It makes me happy, him wanting me to stay. But I know his thoughts drift to *her*, the girl who rescued him. He doesn't know it was me, and so his heart will never truly be mine. If I can tell him the truth, he will love me forever. Moments like this are precisely the sacrifice I make.

I lean my head on his shoulder. I can't be *her*, not to him. But if I remind him of her, maybe in time he will forget her and only see me. He could fall in love with me. I could fall in love with him. With his easy smile and twinkling eyes, the way he holds me, it would be very easy to do.

"I told you earlier that we'd figure out where you would sleep. But I was wondering—" he clears his throat "—if you would sleep in my room?"

Did he just ask me that? I assumed I would be put with another girl in the settlement. If I'm going to anger Mary, this is the quickest way to do it.

He misreads my glance. "No, no, not like that. There aren't beds to spare and most of the girls are already sharing and I didn't think you'd want a big room all to yourself. I asked Jack to put a twin mattress up there by the door. You can sleep in the big bed, and I can sleep by the door. Not a big deal."

His blue eyes are almost black in the dim light. He looks so hungry, so passionate, that I can't turn him down. I nod, my chin quivering. I'm setting myself up to be heartbroken. Why can't I say no?

"I just feel like I need to know everything about you."

Anything but that. That is the one thing I can't give him. His eyes burn mine, and my eyes suddenly feel dry and hot and they start watering. Red skirts the fire and walks up to us then.

"Hey you two. David, we're down to about two weeks of meat. I was thinking we could take a trip up the mountain and go hunting." Red sits down on the log next to us and stretches his legs out toward the fire.

Dave leans away from me. "You hear about the supply drop? Meds. Two days from now."

"Seattle?" Red says, and Dave nods. "That's bad timing."

"Tell me about it."

"Who's going?" Red asks.

"I figured Mary—she knows Seattle better than anyone. I asked Jack but he said no. Funny about it, too."

Red's eyes are steely. "We have to send someone with a tracker. Someone who hasn't been for a while." He looks at his arm. There are nine numbers in silvery ink on a faint ridge of flesh. "I haven't been for eight months. I think it's my turn again. And before you say anything, let's agree. I'm too old. But maybe the scanners won't pay me too much attention."

Dave is about to say more, his mouth in a tight, quivering line. But he doesn't. He stares at Red for a moment then shrugs. "Mary then, you, me, and probably Sam or one of the other guys."

"I think Terra should go too, Dave."

Dave steps back.

Red holds up his hands. "I knew you wouldn't want to. But it'll help things around here. Very few of us trust her. If we take her to Seattle and she doesn't give us away, I think that could say a lot to some people."

Like Mary, I think.

Dave shakes his head, but says, "You're right, Red. I don't like it, but you're right."

"We'll talk about the hunt when we get back," Red says.

Dave nods. I want to unfold the worry and sadness there.

"We could have Terra come along up the mountain, show her where we get the good food." Red smiles. Dave snaps back to attention.

"Terra? Oh yeah, hunting up the mountain. That would be a good idea. We'll definitely need more meat soon, and it'll be fun to show her more of what we do around here. Have you been hunting much?"

I shake my head. I haven't been hunting in my entire life. The only meat we eat in the colony is fish, but those are farm-raised. I have no idea how a wild animal goes from in the wild one moment to lying ready to eat on your plate a little while later.

"Good, then you can come. It's almost thirty miles to the hills, so we always leave early. And we camp out. It's fun, really. Work, but fun."

He smiles, but only with his mouth, not his eyes. The hunting trip does sound like fun. But the supply drop hangs in the air like a thunderhead ready to burst.

ELEVEN

After Dave and I leave the fire, I hear footsteps behind us, and see Mary shadowing us. I stop. I can't let her just follow us upstairs, see us both go into the same room, and then seethe herself to sleep. When I turn, she freezes, the anger and surprise etched in deep furrows between her eyes.

Dave puts a hand to the back of his neck and clears his throat. "Um, well, did you have fun, Mary?"

He hadn't seen her hovering on the edge of the firelight, watching us. I saw the hurt in her eyes, all the while trying to appear stony. I feel bad I cause her so much pain, but I am Dave's friend. I can't just walk away from him.

"What do you think?" She crosses her arms.

"Look, Mary, I'm sorry for whatever it is that's going on here that's hurting your feelings. Really, I am. But that was so long ago—"

Her hands clench. "And what? So easily forgotten? You're such a jerk."

She whirls around, back to the dying fire. Tears glitter on her cheek in the dim light. How much do I really need Dave? If I don't have him, would I hurt as much as she does?

Dave reaches for my hand and leads me up the stairs. In his room, he flops down on the small, dusty mattress by the door and gestures to his bed by the windows. I lie down and look at the ceiling. I can't look at him just now. If I do, all the second thoughts that Mary brings on will be forgotten. I need those second thoughts. I need to stay grounded.

The mattress creaks as Dave shifts his weight. I can feel his eyes on me.

"I'm really sorry Mary is making this hard on you. She's not the easiest person to get along with right now. She has this black and white sense of morality, and there's no middle ground. She can make things difficult."

He really thinks that's the problem? I prop myself up on my elbows. I roll the stump of my tongue around in my mouth. There is so much I need to tell him about how confused I am.

He looks like a lost boy. "That's not what you were thinking?"

I fall back on the bed with a dissatisfied *whump*. He growls in frustration. Then he brings me a paper and pencil.

"So tell me what it is you're feeling."

I clutch the pencil. Telling him the jumble of thoughts in my head doesn't seem like a very good idea. But I promised myself honesty from here on out. Where I come from is the only lie I'll tell. I scribble on the paper, wad it up and chuck it at him. He irons it out and brings a candle close to it.

"You really think she's still in love with me?"

I raise an eyebrow. Is he really that dense?

120

"But she couldn't be. Not after being away for so long and everything that happened. No—she couldn't still be. I'm positive."

What does he think happened in Seattle? From everything Nell told me, it wasn't pretty. I motion for the paper and he tosses it back.

Then why is she so angry at me?

"I don't know—she doesn't trust you. Nell did say she had a rough time in Seattle. Maybe she just doesn't trust strangers any more."

You just don't see it. It's more than that. She's jealous of me. For nothing, though. We're only friends.

His eyes shoot up. I can't tell if he's hurt by the last sentence or just realizes the truth about Mary. I'm afraid to ask.

"So did you have anyone back in Arizona? Anyone that tempted you to stay?"

My first thought races to Jessa. If I knew she wouldn't be okay without me, I would have sacrificed my dream for her. I ache to know if she and Brant are okay, if they're on the Juice Deck kissing or down on Field #3 tending the corn. If they've found some new place to go on a date that no one has thought of yet. If she is happy.

But that isn't what he's asking. I grab the pencil. Unexpected regret twinges in my stomach as I realize Matt would have loved to make me happy. But why in the world am I thinking about this now? My perfectly happy day is turning into confused mush.

"Matt? Doesn't sound like you guys were too serious."

No, he was definitely more enthusiastic than I was.

Dave laughs and sets the paper aside. Then he coughs and the mood deepens like the dark around us. I lie down and pull the thin blanket up around me.

"The supply drop will be dangerous," Dave says. "I don't want to take you, but I think Red's right. Just promise me you'll be careful."

I grunt to him, and stagger into sleep with worry lines etched on my face.

The next day Red finds me behind the school, melting wax from the beehives to make candles. All the power stations are government operated, and the settlement doesn't want to draw attention by sucking electricity, so all their light comes from candles. I stir with a big paddle the way Nell showed me. She is a few feet off, trimming string she found in some blinds in one of the town's houses.

"You ever shot a gun before, Terra?" Red asks, watching the paddle go round and round the big pot of wax.

I shake my head.

"If you're coming tomorrow, I think you should learn. Everyone else here at least knows how to fire a gun, even if they don't do it on a regular basis. You got to learn to be careful with a weapon, and got to know how to protect yourself."

I understand the reasoning, but I'm not so sure I trust myself. Mr. Klein told plenty of stories about how dangerous guns are. I thought of him that first day on the beach when I saw Mary throw hers to the ground. Guns are delicate weapons, easily misused. I shudder.

"I can understand if you don't want to. Lots of people feel the same way. But it's necessary, you see. Everyone needs to know how to use a gun to defend themselves and get food. And everyone going on the supply drops needs to be ready to use one."

His gray eyes study me very closely and very deeply. I'm not comfortable under his gaze. He, more than anyone else here, could figure out the secrets I'm hiding just by looking at me long enough. Even though I don't feel it, I nod my head resolutely.

"Good then. As soon as you're done helping out my Nell, why don't you meet me on the steps and I'll teach you a few things."

He saunters away, slightly favoring his left leg. Nell watches him go with a fond smile. She ties the strings to several long sticks.

"He's a good man." She brings the sticks over to the pot.

We slowly dip one stick of strings into the pot and raise it up, then balance it on the backs of two chairs. The first layer of about a hundred for this set of candles.

"He wants to keep us all safe, and I know it's getting harder on him as he gets older. He still has that same sense of chivalry he had when he found me near Seattle."

We dip another set of strings. I look at her and raise my eyebrows.

"What happened in Seattle?"

I nod. More importantly, I want to know what happened to Mary in Seattle, and I hope the conversation leads that way.

Nell's eyes glaze for a moment, and she lets the strings sag. I motion that it's alright. If this is too painful a memory, she doesn't have to tell me.

"No, no, Terra. It's fine. I just haven't talked about it for so long. I was twenty when I decided to leave Seattle. I had lived there almost my whole life with my mother and father and two older brothers. We lived in an abandoned apartment building with a few other families. The scanners recorded our movements every day. If someone didn't report to work in the morning, an agent collected them and took them to a camp. All the watchers—"

I held my breath. They called the cameras watchers too.

"—were rewired from local law enforcement. The feed goes directly to the capitol. No one trusted each other. Not even the families who lived together. No one knew who was an agent and who wasn't. Food was scarce. If you happened to scrounge up more food, plant more food, catch more food—however you came upon it—in the morning it might be missing if you weren't careful. Everything was looted and windows were smashed. The military did very little about it. They didn't care about buildings. They just cared about people's loyalties. And hungry people were dependent on the supply drops.

"It was quiet because there weren't very many people, not like when the city was alive. But it wasn't a peaceful quiet, not like here. Cars were left in the middle of the street, abandoned, doors and windows hanging open. It was an unfriendly, scary kind of quiet. You never knew who was watching you. You felt nervous just walking down the street, no matter what time of day it was. My father never let any of us go out by ourselves. We always had to go out together.

"One night my father and brothers came home with big sacks full of food. They had found a basement under one of the buildings that hadn't yet been looted. They had found all kinds of canned food. We hid it away in a corner like we always did.

124

"That night, I woke up to the smell of burning. Our building was on fire. I couldn't see through the smoke, and it filled my lungs and I couldn't breathe. All I could think of was finding a way out. I finally managed to escape, and when I got outside, I saw another of the families that lived in our building. They had stolen all of the food from our hiding place and lit the building on fire. They thought we should have shared our find with them. But they had never shared anything with us! Their oldest daughter saw me crawl out a window. She pulled out a knife and came after me with it. I managed to scramble away and escape. But I was never able to come back and try to help my family. They all died in the building that night."

Nell sits down for a minute in one of the chairs that holds the dipped strings. I kneel down on the ground beside her and put a hand on her knee. But she isn't crying.

"I have no more tears for that night. They ran out a long time ago. But my heart still aches every time I think of it."

I lay my head on her knee and she runs her fingers through my hair.

"I decided to leave Seattle and find somewhere else, someplace where the quiet was peaceful. I was terrified to leave. I had never been alone before, and I knew if I got caught, I would be better off dead. The first thing I did was cut out my tracker. Red found me that way, covered with blood and carving my tracker to pieces. I was so scared of him. His hair and beard were flaming red and long and wiry and sticking out in every direction. I thought he was a demon. But he saw how spooked I was, like a cat, and never came nearer to me than we are to that pot. He started slow. He could see it was something that would take time. But he would talk to me for hours, telling me stories. I wouldn't say, couldn't say much to him. It was still too fresh. But he didn't seem to mind. It reminds me a lot of you and David." A smile tweaks the corners of her mouth.

"And so we wandered together. And by the time we found ourselves at this settlement, I had fallen in love with him. Dear man." With those words, a tear slips from the corner of her eyes and down her cheek to fall on mine. She can cry tears of happiness now. I squeeze her leg, letting her know how much I enjoy her happiness. She laughs and shoos me off so we can finish another few rounds with the candles.

"We can't hope to get these done today, but I'm sure someone else will help me with them while you're gone."

I stir the pot again.

"And Terra? Please be gentle with Mary. She went through a lot in Seattle. I think she had romantic notions of helping establish the city back to the way it was. And if it was just the city, maybe she could. But that's not where the problem starts. She found out it's not much different from when I was there. She's lucky to be back here."

Unexpectedly, I feel sorry for Mary. I don't know the details of her wounds, but I can't blame her for being angry. Dave is the one thing she trusted, and things just haven't been quite right between them since she came back.

After several more dips into the pot of wax, Nell says I should go see Red. I groan as I walk around to the front steps of the school. I really don't want to learn to shoot a gun. If everyone around here learned at one time or another, then there are more than enough people to cover the bases.

Red sits on the steps, sipping a glass of water and looking to the horizon where you can just see the thin ribbon of the Sound through the trees.

"So you've never even held a gun?" he asks as I sit next to him. I shake my head.

"That by your own choosing?"

I look at my mud-caked boots. Not really, there are no guns in the colony. But if I had been given the chance, I would have turned it down.

"I can understand that you're nervous about it. I can respect that. But guns are important to survival around here. You've got to understand how to handle one. Especially since you're coming tomorrow. We'll each have one, including you, and you need to know how to use it."

I will carry a gun? He watches me, studying my face. He looks back east and takes another sip of water, and then stands up slowly, his joints popping. There is a rifle on the steps. Red grips it and starts south.

"There's a field a few hundred yards off where we can practice. Follow me."

Not a request, an order. I know Red can feel the anxiety rolling off of me, and he takes deft control of the situation. I have to follow him. My limbs feel wooden as I plod after him through the waist-high grass and scrub.

The sun settles toward the west, and the only salvation I can hope for is dinner in an hour. Until then, I am stuck out here with Red and a gun.

The grass in the field is shorter and the trees are sparse. Targets hang from the branches and shells litter the ground.

"We come through and clean those up once in a while. We can manage to repack 'em. Found a few tools for it in a town not far from here. Boring, tedious job. But sometimes that's just the thing you need around here. Now watch. You'll only get one chance. We don't want to draw attention with too many gun shots."

Red carefully turns off what he calls the safety. He makes a deliberate show of always pointing the gun away from me. Then he brings the rifle up to his shoulder and wedges it tight against the joint. He points to a sack full of holes hanging from a tree.

"Cover your ears."

I stuff my fingers in both ears and squint. I don't want to watch, but I know I have to. This lesson will never end if I don't pay attention.

The sound makes me jump. It sounds worse than the thunder the night I slept outside the school. Red's shoulder jars back slightly, and I keep my eyes on the bag. It spins as another hole pocks the fabric.

"Once you're done, flip the safety again. Always remember whether the safety is on or off. Always."

I nod, my hands still against my ears. Red laughs.

"You okay, Terra?"

I am still staring open-mouthed at the bag. He nudges my shoulder.

"Uhh?" is all I can manage.

"You ready for your turn?"

I shake my head. I don't want to touch that thing.

"Now I know you're nervous and heaven knows what's made you that way, but you're going to learn if it's the last thing I do. If you come tomorrow, you're learning, and that's final."

I lower my hands and nod. I reach for the gun. Red places it in my hands and doesn't let go until my fingers are wrapped securely around it. He makes sure I'm not pointing it at him. Or at me. He helps me raise it up against my shoulder.

"Now tuck it in there nice and tight. This girl's got some kick and you don't want to have a bruised shoulder keeping you home."

I nod and hold the butt firmly against my shoulder. I feel like I'll dislocate my shoulder if I hold it there any tighter.

"Now turn off the safety."

With a click I turn it off. I feel like I have a snake in my hands and if I let go, it'll bite me.

"Now sight along the length of the barrel. Try for the bag in the closest tree. Hold it steady, and when you're ready, ease on the trigger."

I look down the long, dark shaft of metal at the bag hanging in the tree. It is a hundred feet away. I gaze at it until the sweat drips in my eyes. The bag hardly moves but it seems impossible to hit.

Red clears his throat. "Any time now, Terra."

How long have I been standing here? I can do this. I am still alive after the past few days, and I can do anything. I take one last look at the bag, then close my eyes.

The force of the shot knocks me backward and Red scrambles away. As soon as I realize I'm not shot, I let go of the gun and lie with my eyes shut, listening to my heart race.

"You okay?"

I see Red's shadow through my red eyelids. I put my hands over my face. My shoulder aches, but I nod.

"Then next time why don't you try keeping your eyes open?"

Next time? Surely there won't be a next time?

"You can't hope to hit anything if you don't open your eyes. Best as I can figure, that bullet made it all the way to the Sound."

I laugh then, and when Red realizes I'm not insane, he joins in. "Maybe next time you could try a hand gun. A bit easier to manage."

A gun in any form will be torture, but easier to manage would definitely be an improvement. I just hope I don't have to use it tomorrow.

TWELVE

Dave shakes me awake. I dreamed of guns and blood last night. Guns that felt like ice in my hands; blood that dripped from a ragged slash in a white arm. Waking up is a relief. The corner of the heavy drape weaves in the breeze, and the air cools my sweaty skin. Then I remember we are going to Seattle this morning, and I'm not sure if I want to sleep or wake. There is a coil of rope in my stomach that pulls tighter and tighter.

Breakfast is somber. Everyone looks at me. Everyone looks at Mary, Dave, Red, and Sam, the other boy who agreed to come. They look at us like they would a funeral procession. But Nell holds Red's hand and pats his whiskered cheek. Tears shine in her eyes, but she smiles.

"Come back to me tomorrow," she says. "I need help with the candles."

His lips brush hers, and he pulls her fiercely against him.

"I'll help you, Nellie girl. So don't do it all without me."

She lingers in his arms and then pulls back. Nell holds my hand and smiles, and I feel more lonely than I have since I've been here. I feel like she's trying to say goodbye and good luck all at once.

The sky is still dark and we load into a sleek boat painted the same gray color as the water. Most of the settlement is on the rocky shore to see us off. They stand huddled up against the water's edge. No one speaks. Jack stands a few feet apart and waves once. A gun goes in for each of us, a pack of food, a gray blanket too huge for one person. I don't try to ask what it's for. I sit next to Mary, and I don't want to look like I'm prying for secrets. Whatever she may think, I am not one of "them."

Sam starts the motor and the boat lurches out into the sound. We need to get to Seattle before the sun bounces off the water, before someone watching will see our boat. We huddle under the blanket, and the blanket turns us the same color as the water. Only Sam stands above the itchy cloth.

"It's a little more than five miles across the Sound," Dave yells above the engine and the spray. "Get comfy, it'll take a little while."

I shiver. The morning is wet and cold. I was getting used to being so warm I sweated all the time here. Now I'm cold again, and the cold sharpens my mind and sharpens the fear. I try to think warm thoughts. I shove the blanket up tight around my chin.

Red rubs his right arm. The tracker lump moves under his fingers as he massages the skin.

"You get your tracker scanned to get supplies," he says. "So one of us always goes to a supply drop. We spread it out as much as we can, so one person doesn't get noticed."

132

I nod. Even getting necessary medical supplies is a danger-ous job. Everyone goes back to looking straight ahead as the skyline full of broken buildings like jagged teeth grows imper-ceptibly larger. Their silhouettes brighten as the dawn pushes forward.

Mary leans her head toward me. Her hair whips her face so she can't look at me. "It doesn't have to be this way."

I shake my head. What is she talking about?

"I don't know if I can trust you. I wish I could, but I can't. When you're used to being beaten for not stealing enough food, when you're used to being locked up in a dark room all by your-self and hearing the agents searching all around you, well. Yeah, I don't know if I can trust you. I'd like to. Dave obviously does." She looks at him, and her eyes change. They are so full of long-ing I almost choke on it. Some of the softness lingers as she holds her hair back with one hand and turns to me.

"Terra, I'm sorry for everything. Really. I just can't stand the thought of an outsider right now. Things are too precarious. Too carefully balanced and then wham! You come along and I'm afraid it's all going to come crashing down."

I want to put a hand on her arm. That's what I would have done for Jessa. For any friend. But I can't with her. She needs Dave to do it. But he won't, either. Instead I say nothing and stare straight ahead. The wind stings my eyes.

We reach Seattle just as the sun peaks behind a building and the hazy beams glint off broken glass, splitting shards of light into a hundred directions. It would be beautiful if it weren't skeletons of buildings that the sun shines on.

"Will we see anyone?" Dave asks. Mary shakes her head.

"No, we shouldn't. Not until we're closer to the drop site."
But she cranes her neck around anyway, scanning the streets
that finger out toward the water from between buildings. I see
no one.

An old, ruined pier floats crazily in front of us. Sam navi-
gates the boat underneath the pier and stops against a wooden
post closest to land. We knock against it a few times as he
throws a line around and secures us. I carry my gun above my
head like everyone else does. Sam stays with the boat, but the
rest of us jump into the waist-deep water. I clench my teeth. I
will be walking in these wet clothes all morning. I shiver and
wade to shore.

"Sam's here until midnight," Dave says. The others nod.
This is obviously the plan for every time they've done this. Dave
looks at me and his eyes cloud. I nod too. "At midnight he
leaves. If someone isn't here, he leaves. So get here by midnight."

They tuck their guns into their waistbands under their
shirts. I do too. Red wears an empty pack on his back—the biggest one we could scrounge up in the settlement. He leads the
way through the streets. Mary is close behind him, whispering
directions. Dave scans the streets, the rooftops, the windows in
buildings. I'm not sure what he's looking for, but it makes my
skin crawl and I start looking, too.

We walk through the ghost streets and see no one. A rustle
comes from a cross street and I whirl toward it, half wrenching
my gun out. But a cat slinks from a door swinging open and
closed and an empty can rolls out the door after it. My hand
trembles as I try to shove my gun back under my shirt. Dave
touches my arm to steady me.

134

"Calm down. It's illegal to have guns. Keep it hidden unless absolutely necessary. Especially when we get closer."

We reach a wide swathe of concrete that stretches as far as I can see north and south and looms below us like a moat. Cars with smashed glass line the bottom. The crumbling remains of a bridge jut out at our feet and from the other side of the road. An old metal sign dangles on the edge of the bridge, a faded white five on a blue insignia.

People gather on the other side, near a white brick building with a peaked roof and tall chimney. Several men dressed all in black and wearing helmets stand on the roof of the building. They each hold a gun, and the guns are pointed at the crowd. Red told me never to point my gun at someone unless I plan to shoot them. I bounce on my toes, ready to flee back down the street we came from.

But Red starts climbing down into the pit of cars. Surely he can't go down alone, not without help. Why aren't Dave and Mary following? I shove the rising panic back down my throat and start toward him, but Mary grabs my arm.

"No, he goes by himself from here. None of us have trackers. We're illegal." She pulls me behind an overgrown tree that shields the three of us from those on the other side. I crouch between two roots that raise canyons in the sidewalk.

Red shouldn't be going down there. I can't help thinking he's too old to be doing it. He's too kind. And he has Nell. Nell needs him. He's too vulnerable down among the twisted metal and broken glass. Those sharp things could pierce him. I remember my dreams of blood. I squeeze my eyes closed and open them again. A few men on the other side notice him, and they laugh.

"Hey, grandpa!" one calls. He has black hair and a sickly pallor to his skin. His eyes are rimmed in dark circles. He jabs a friend in the ribs. "Don't you think you should just stay down there with all the relics? We'll get your supplies for you. Safer that way, don't you think? No one comes from that side of the city unless I know about it."

I bristle and the anger makes me brave for a single second. The one with black hair sneers. I don't like the hungry look on his face. But Mary still holds my arm.

"Don't say anything. They're dangerous, all of them. Red has done this before. This isn't the part we have to worry about."

The guys jeer a little more, until a soldier comes over and jabs the barrel of his rifle right in the chest of the black-haired one. The sun glances off the soldier's visor, and I can barely make out features. I wonder if he's even human. I can't hear what the soldier says, but each one of the guys shows him their right forearms. The soldier waves over a young woman dressed in a suit. Her blond hair is pulled back so tightly at first I think she's bald. As soon as she appears, one of them tries to disappear in the crowd, but another soldier standing by grabs him and wrenches his left arm behind his back. The other soldier squeezes his right forearm so tightly the skin bulges on either side of his glove.

The woman waves a small machine over their arms. Each one lights up a faint blue color, and she reads whatever information displays on the screen. But the one who tried to escape, his arm doesn't glow blue. She swipes the machine over his arm one more time. His face is ashen. Then she flicks two fingers, and the soldiers throw him to the ground. One stomps a boot

136

on his face and grinds his cheek into the pavement. I can't turn away. I watch blood spurt out of his nose, and I can't turn away.

The woman speaks, her face disinterested and not looking at him, using a stylus on the screen of her little machine that decides his fate. He tries to speak, but he can't with the boot pressed into his face. Then she nods and the soldiers drag him up. The crowd parts as the soldiers take him to a truck outside the mob of people. The guy's head lolls on his shoulders. Everyone is silent as they watch him go. As soon as he is inside the back of the truck and the doors close, they resume. Like they were on pause for three seconds and then real life starts again.

I turn to Dave. He's pale, and his eyes flash with so many emotions I couldn't even begin to name them. Mary's eyes are stony. She's lived among them. She's probably seen this many times. I look at her arm. She has a jagged scar that's still pink and puckered. She had a tracker too, and like Nell, she must have cut hers out.

Getting hauled away is a risk we all take.

Red is up on the other side of the interstate now. The man without a tracker created enough of a distraction that no one else notices him arrive. He hovers on the edges of the crowd.

A huge truck with rows of wheels pulls up, beeping. People slowly move out of the way, and more soldiers appear to form a perimeter around the truck. They jab at the crowd and the crowd falls back.

The back of the truck swings open. The inside is lined with rows and rows of boxes on shelves, and a man in a suit almost identical to the woman's sits in a wheeled chair behind a desk. Two young men in gray jumpsuits stand behind him with their hands behind their backs. The woman stands on the ground in front of the desk, flanked by two soldiers.

An amplified voice speaks. "Welcome, citizens of New America, to your monthly supply replenishment. This month, we provide you with medicine and first-aid supplies. Remember, if you or someone you know is critically ill, bring them to the free clinic behind Town Hall."

Mary snorts. "Yeah, and you'll never see them again."

"Show your personal identification chip to the verifier. Then you will receive your supply box. Once you receive your box, please leave the premises. If anyone tries to obtain supplies illegally, you will be detained."

"Permanently," Mary whispers.

I wonder again why I'm here. Dave watches Red's every move. Will he burst from our cover if something happens to him? Could we even do anything to save him? None of us have trackers, and from what I've seen, that marks you. Fatally.

But Red knows what he's doing. People shove to get closer to the front. A soldier steps in and breaks things up with a quick swipe of a rifle barrel. Then they fall in a line, and it's mostly orderly. Red stays around the fringes, looking down, not meeting anyone's eyes. It's like he's not there at all. No one else without a tracker is found.

When a young woman with a bruise covering the whole left side of her face gets a supply box, her eyes flick around and she slinks away down a street darkened by tall buildings. Once in the alley, I see a shadow kick her legs out from under her, swipe the box, and disappear into the darkness. She falls on her face and sobs. But she is out of sight from the soldiers, and there's nothing she can do.

138

For the first time since I came here, I want to go back to the colony. I can deal with the stuff I hated. It might eat me up inside, but I can do it. I want to live where Mr. Klein can get me some aloe without having to assault anyone. Where the corridors are well-lit and I don't cower from shadows. Where I don't look over my shoulder while I'm walking into the Juice Deck.

I want to be safe.

Then Mary grips my arm. She doesn't realize she's doing it. I look up, and Red stands in front of the woman. He holds out his arm, and she scans it. His arm flashes blue. She studies the screen, glancing at Red. She asks him a question. He shrugs. A long moment passes. What are they doing up there? I scrape my palms along my pants. The soldier next to Red takes a shuffle step and I almost burst from the tree and hurl myself across the interstate. But Dave keeps his hand firmly on my shoulder. Then the woman hands the screen to the man at the desk. He taps his lips and speaks. Red answers. The two in gray jumpsuits turn and get supply boxes off the shelves. They hand them to Red. He puts the boxes in the pack and slings it on his back.

The black-haired guy watches him, the red mouth in his sickly face twitching. Red turns, nudging through the thinning crowd and keeping his head down as he saunters away from the violence of the supply drop. But he doesn't come back over the interstate. He turns down another street.

"He's got it," Dave says. "Let's go. Mary, keep your eyes on him. Terra, follow me."

We stay low and dart from tree to tree along the interstate, parallel to the path Red takes. Mary keeps one hand on the gun at her back and watches Red make his way down the street. But

I still feel too far from him. Broken concrete litters the sidewalk. I jump over it as best I can, but my boots weigh me down and I'm clumsy. Red doesn't glance at us at all. We aren't together.

I see a waver of movement from a window two stories up. A girl is there, watching us. She might be twelve. Her brown hair hangs limp around her face. She waves someone else to the window. A man joins her, and they look down at Red. One of them puts a walkie-talkie to his mouth. I point to them.

"They're watching him," Dave says. Mary nods and her hands turn white as they tighten around her gun. I glance back the way we came. We've already gone a block. There's no one behind us, but the black-haired man is a ways behind Red, walking casually with his hands in his pockets. He kicks a chunk of broken concrete. It skitters across the sidewalk and onto the road, and he never looks away from Red. He doesn't care about us—we don't have supply boxes. I can't tell if Red knows he's there, but his face is drawn and his eyes are wide. He looks about to catch us out of the corner of his eyes, but he doesn't let himself.

"He's going to panic," Mary says.

Dave keeps walking. "He's fine. He's done this before. He'll be fine." He prods me along. The worry is overwhelming, but I can't look at Red. We're not together.

"Turn south here and the building is just on the corner," Mary hisses.

A rendezvous point. The bridge over the interstate is passable here. We duck behind an awning and wait. Mary stands next to me. Dave looks past the corner. My heart slams against my ribs as I watch Red walk alone across the bridge. The black-haired man doesn't close the gap. The path we've chosen is too

140

exposed, and he's making sure we're well enough away from the supply drop before he attacks. He slinks along like a panther.

I shudder the length of my body. My hands shake so badly I take them off the gun in my waistband. I can't be trusted with a weapon. I barely know how to use it. The violence of half an hour ago catches up with me, and the sweat pours down my face even though I feel cold. Small pings of light hover around the edges of my vision. I put a hand out to steady myself.

"Dave, I don't know if she can make it." Mary actually looks concerned. Dave glances back at me. He puts both hands on my shoulders and stoops down to look in my face.

"You okay, Terra?"

I almost scream when he touches me, and I smack a hand over my mouth. I shake my head. I am far from okay.

"Why'd I listen to him? I knew it was too much too soon."

Mary peers around the corner. "Red's across. On our side of the street now. Time to move."

I can't look away from Dave's eyes. They draw me in. There has to be some calm there I can borrow. He doesn't blink but stares at me. My heart slows in my chest and I try to breathe deeply. Don't look away from me, I beg silently. But he can't look at me forever. He tears his eyes from mine to follow Red. My breath hitches again.

"We have to move now, Terra." Dave slips his hands off my shoulders. He grabs my hand too hard and pulls me away from the building. My fingers ache but I don't want him to loosen his grip. It helps hold me together. My legs follow him, but I can't feel them. My whole body is going numb.

We're in a canyon of buildings so tall the clouds look small above them. All the windows are blown out and some of the roofs are ragged. Glass crunches under our feet. Red walks two hundred feet behind us, but I can't see the black-haired man anywhere. Then Mary nods and we hunch through a broken hole in a door and wait. A minute later, Red crawls through.

He's sweaty and a little pale, but fine. Scared, though. Just like me.

"I forgot how intense it is," he says as he slips the pack from his shoulders and slumps to the floor. He holds his head in his hands. Mary offers him her canteen and he takes a drink. I hear him swallow. The quiet around us is suffocating. Dim light shines through windows and lights squares across the floor littered with glass and boards as far as I can see.

"How long we staying?" Red asks.

"Until dark," Dave says.

Mary takes the canteen back. "They won't be able to see us as easily. Hopefully we can slip away before they find us." Mary looks down and scuffs the floor with her shoe. "Med drop is always rough—worse than any other. People care more about drugs than they do about food. I didn't like the look of that dark-haired guy. You could tell he's been on it for a while. He's the dangerous one. Terra, did you see him following us?"

I nod frantically. My body is still laced with adrenaline and I can't do anything small.

"Where?"

I open her hand. *I saw him until we hid the first time.*

"He might not know we're here," she says. "But I doubt it. Always doubt it. We'll need to keep watch at the door. This is obviously some kind of territory for him. He'll know it better than we do."

Dave offers first watch. He stands at the door and with the light streaming in, I can't see anything more than his black silhouette. I lean my head back against a cinderblock wall. I want to cry. My longing for the colony overwhelms me. Mary sits down beside me. I wish she were Jessa.

She looks at her hands. "I don't know where you're from, but it's obviously different than here. You act like you've never seen anyone beaten, never seen anyone killed. But you had your tongue hacked out. I guess we've all been brutalized no matter where we're from. I'm not sure what's worse, losing your tongue or being used to seeing people get hurt like that."

She lays her gun across her knees. "My family—why do I still call them that?—the people I stayed with here, they would lock me in a janitor's closet. My job was to steal other people's supplies. I was pretty, I was small. I guess they thought I'd be good at it. I couldn't bring myself to hurt other people, so I'd beg. I'd never bring back enough to please them. So they'd lock me in the closet. It was one building over from where they lived, and it was abandoned. They cut out my tracker not long after I started. They didn't want an agent to find me and be able to trace me back to them. So they hacked it out of me and stitched me up."

She runs her fingers over the lumpy scar. I can't help staring at it. I was wrong about her tracker. Had they used anesthetic? Had they pinned her down?

She glances quickly at Dave. "The closet was always dark. The building would groan, and I would sit crouched in the corner thinking it would crash down on me at any second. Then I would hear the footsteps outside. Heavy boots and the click of high heels. Agents were out there. I knew if they found me, they would take me away and no one would ever see me again. I couldn't cry because I didn't want to make noise. I thought of Dave every day."

Her eyes glisten, but she brings the neck of her shirt up to her face before the tears spill over. I sit awkwardly next to her and put a hand on her arm. I don't touch the scar. I feel ashamed for having thought badly of her. Of course she doesn't trust me; she's hard-wired not to. And then she came back to the settlement only to find Dave wasn't there when she needed him. How messed up all our lives are.

I can't make out the details of him as he stands darkened by the light behind him, but I trace the profile with my eyes. The firm jaw, broad shoulders. The longish hair and straight nose. He is strong. No wonder she leaned on him. But what changed for him? Why does he push her away? And again I feel hopeful. He lets me lean on him. That knowledge will have to be enough to bury the thoughts of the colony. It will have to be, or I might not make it out of Seattle alive.

The light shifts across the floor as the sun sets. The day was quiet. Two people had passed the door, but neither of them had been the black-haired man, and they hadn't shown any interest.

As dusk creeps on, we stand up and stretch. Dave offers us some old bread from the pack. We each take a swig from the canteen. Then as soon as the sun is completely down and the street is more shadow than light, Dave sticks his head out the door. The street is violet gray and barren.

"Quiet now," Mary says. "We're out after curfew."

I don't want to know what the punishment is if we're caught.

We file out. This time, they take out their guns and make no show of hiding them. I reach for mine, and my hands tremble as I take it out and hold it at my side.We stick to the sides of buildings where awnings and overhangs hide us occasionally. Not enough to make me comfortable. Clouds blanket the moon, but it still feels too bright. Every so often we pause, listening for footsteps. None come.

Then I hear the whirring chop of a helicopter. My feet freeze to the ground, unable to move. The others hear it, and urge me forward. A helicopter bursts over the top of a building with a single beam of light swinging across the street.

"We can't stop now, Terra!" Dave pushes me forward. He's rough but I know the urgency behind it. There are agents up there, looking for people just like us. My bare arm almost glows in the night. It's unblemished. What would they think of that? I've never even had a tracker. There are a few people like that at the settlement, and I know they will never be asked to go to a supply drop.

We are almost to the pier and we jog faster. The helicopter retreats back away from the water. Red pants next to me, the pack tugging on his shoulders. Dave leads. Mary comes behind us, turning every few seconds to glance behind. We cut over on the next north-south street to go back where we started, and I see the long dark line of pier slice into the water. Dark shadows rise up were the pier meets the street.

"Thought you'd come back this way," drawls the black-haired man. His face is rugged with shadows, carving deep lines into his cheeks. "It's been a while since I've seen someone come across the water for a drop. Wonder if you're part of the same group. You have some camp across the sound? I'd be interested in that."

Two other men stand behind him. They hold long objects in their hands. I pray they aren't guns. One of them slaps his against a palm. Clubs, then.

We stop, and Dave raises his gun in front of him, aimed right at Black Hair's chest. The smile slips off his face. They hadn't seen our guns.

"Where'd you get that? Not included in the standard supply drops. I could report you to an agent, you know. You'd all be dead by morning." He isn't smiling any more, but he isn't falling back, either.

Then Mary steps next to Dave and points her gun as well. The men step back.

"It's a regular army, isn't it?" Black Hair sneers, but stands aside.

"He'll report us," Mary whispers. "He'll report us and then they'll come."

"A risk we'll take," Dave says. "I'm not risking gunshots so close to the city. Not unless they attack us."

Dave walks stiffly and we follow. We make a wide berth around the three men. Dave never takes his gun off Black Hair. We walk down under the pier and slip into the water. Sam breathes a heavy sigh when he sees us, and heaves us into the boat. I never noticed how young he is—younger than me. How long has he been down here hiding while Black Hair stood up there waiting? Sam starts the motor and guns it out from under the pier and into the deep water.

As soon as we're free from the pier, Black Hair bolts and jumps down into the water. What is he doing? Then I hear the roar of another motor. The boat pulls alongside him, and he pulls himself in. This boat isn't dull gray like ours, it's silver and all reflections.

"They're following!" Sam shouts.

"Just drive! But stay close to the city. He still doesn't know what direction we came from. I don't want them thinking we're escaping west," Dave says above the motor. "We'll take care of them."

Red and Mary both have rifles out and steadied on the side of the boat. I can't even grip my gun properly. I hunker down against the side, put my gun next to me, and cover my ears. It's all too loud: the motors, the sea spray, the gun fire as it explodes across the water. I jar against the side of the boat as we lurch across the waves. I'll have bruises in a few hours.

Then comes a whir faster than I can breathe and I see a bullet hole in the side of the boat where one hadn't been before. Right next to my head.

"You okay?" Dave shouts. I can't answer. I could be bleeding and I'd have no idea. He turns from me and shoots back at the boat that comes closer and closer as we bob and weave along the shoreline.

The silver boat is right behind us and Sam panics. He turns the wheel too sharply. Red, Dave, and Mary are all thrown into the middle of the boat, a tangle of limbs and no one can reach a gun. I look back, and in the darkness I'm sure the shadow standing in the other boat is Black Hair with a rifle pointed right at Sam's back.

I fight back the nausea and pick up my gun. My hands shake so badly I can't even aim straight. All I want to do is close my eyes and fall asleep. Wake up in my white, sterile bed in my temperature-controlled quarters. To forget this ever happened. Aiming a gun at someone's chest is so wrong, I can't even breathe.

"Shoot him!" Red bellows, still grappling for his gun. "Terra, just shoot him! Pretend he's a bag hanging in a tree."

But pretending this man in front of me is a bag hanging in a tree is even more wrong than aiming the gun at him. How did I get here?

Then my finger brushes against the trigger and all is silent around me. I hear only the motor from the other boat and the water lapping the sides of mine. My finger arches against the trigger and I'm about to let out my breath one more time and squeeze when a shaft of light brighter than a comet tail shines down on the silver boat. I shield my eyes and look up. A helicopter.

Instinctively I drop down, and I'm covered with the gray blanket. Sam has cut the motor and we drift away, rolling across the swells, all of us breathing heavily under the cloth. I peek from under an edge.

"Lower your weapons." It's the same amplified voice as at the supply drop. Does it always sound the same?

Black Hair and the others point their guns at the helicopter and fire. It's a death wish, but I guess being out on the water at night, guns in hand, already doomed them. A machine gun lets out a spattering of firework pops and they all fall away. Soon their boat falls away as well.

148

The helicopter hovers for a few minutes more, watching the boat sink beneath the water. Then it turns toward the city and the chopping whir fades into the night. The water and sky all around us are silent and dark. All I can see are the helicopters circling the city in the night, their lights searching for more death.

We drift for a while. None of us wants to start the motor. We lie in the bottom of the boat, all of us lined next to each other like fish on a platter, and none of us wants to move. Every time I close my eyes, I see the burst of light from gunfire. It burns my eyes.

After an eternity, after my back has ached for so long it's numb, Sam finally pulls back the blanket. Seattle is small on the horizon. The lights from the helicopters still circle the sky, but they are too far away. The motor roars to life and we sprint for home.

Dawn just turns the sky gray when we bump into the shore. Jack is asleep on the ground, wrapped in a blanket. As soon as the boat scuds on the rocks, his eyes fly open and he stands up, rushing forward. Red laughs. Now that we can laugh.

"Easy there, son."

Jack laughs too, embarrassed. But then he hollers. "Nell, he's back!"

Nell appears and races to Red's arms. She buries her face in his shirt and he holds her so tightly I think they might never come apart again. He nestles his cheek into her silver hair. Then he cries.

I didn't know Red could cry. But now he does. Now that we're away from the city and the agents and the people and we're safe and there's time for crying. Dave and Mary turn away to give them some privacy. Dave hands Jack the supply pack.

"I hope it's all in there. We should go in and catalog it and put it away."

"Yes, first thing. Then you need to talk about a hunting trip. Everyone in there is about to go insane with worry. A hunting trip is a distraction. They all need that right now."

Dave nods and walks with Jack into the school. I'm left with Mary. She no longer looks at me with cold fury. She is merely wary.

"Come on, let's go in. I'm starved."

Breakfast isn't ready yet, but someone scrounges each of us up a plate. Stale bread, over-ripe strawberries, and salted fish, and I can only taste the ghosts of flavors. The five of us who went on the supply drop sit at a table and eat, while everyone else grabs a chair and circles us. They all want the story.

Between bites, the others take turns telling. I just look at my plate and eat one mechanical bite after another. My stomach clenches, and I'm glad I can't taste the food. I shiver when Red tells them his version—when he was across the impossibly wide chasm of ruined cars, and we wouldn't be able to get to him in time if something went wrong. The rest feels like a dream to my too tired body. An ugly dream. But I feel the ache in my spine, the bruises on my shoulders, and I know it is not.

I am shaken from my stupor by laughter. How had this started? I didn't even notice the mood had shifted.

Dave stands before all of us, mock-holding a rifle, aiming along its invisible barrel. Jack runs the length of the room, and then Dave makes a shooting noise and Jack falls.

I am horrified. What are they playing at?

"That was how I got that grizzly on the last trip. Sure he was a small one, but it was a grizzly. Who's coming tomorrow?"

Hunting. Not murder. I sigh. I need to go somewhere quiet for a few hours and clear my head. I leave the cafeteria and the laughter, the hunt planning, the hugs, and the relief that is so strong I can touch it with my hands.

I climb the stairs, and I think I might collapse before I make it to the top. So I slump onto the landing and sit, looking back at the cafeteria doors and the light that spills through them and the voices that echo up to me on the stairs.

I lean my head back on the railing, and finally the tears slip out. I am safe, I am fed, and now I can cry. I'm about to lie down when the door swings open. Jack sees me.

"Mind if I join you?"

I wipe my face hard with my hand and shake my head. I don't really want to be alone. The last thing I need is to be alone where all I see is a black boot smashing a face, a girl crying in an alley, and Red walking all alone under the watching buildings.

Jack sits next to me and props his hands on his knees.

"I've never been on a supply drop. I know I'd be no good." He says it matter-of-factly, like he doesn't even mind if I don't ask him why.

"You've never seen anything like that before, have you?"

I shake my head and the tears fall harder. A sob catches in my throat. Jack puts a tentative hand on my shoulder.

"It never gets easy. And that's a good thing."

I lean my head on his hand and cry for a while longer. When the tears have dried up and the gasps between sobs have subsided, he stands and offers his hand. "Come on, I'll help you up to bed."

I'm grateful for him as he guides me up the stairs and into Dave's room.

"There's still an hour or so before the sun's up. Try to sleep."

But I can't. I am afraid of the dreams. Afraid to even close my eyes.

THIRTEEN

I wake up to warm sunlight on my face. I had been dreaming about lying in Field #3 with no protective suit on. My dad had been shaking me awake, crying over my red skin, moaning about what he could have done better. I shudder.

Dave is already gone, the blanket a heap at the foot of his bed.

I shake the sleep from my head. I am so tired. I need to sleep more before the hunting trip tomorrow. But then a flurry of people outside my door—people with packs and supplies and guns—and I wonder if it *is* tomorrow. Have I really slept for an entire day?

I dress and shamble downstairs. Dave is at the bottom, going through packs and checking supplies.

After a breakfast of eggs, strawberries, and bread, those of us going on the hunting trip gather outside the cafeteria.

Dave, Jack, Sam, and eight other men offered to come. I'm the only girl. I don't mind. I know Dave will take good care of me, and Jack is quickly becoming a good friend. Red offered, but Nell wouldn't let him. She still wants him close by after the supply drop.And there are scanner checkpoints along the way. No one with a tracker is allowed to come.

Red must have been right about my going on the supply drop. I don't know the others too well, but they don't bat an eye when Dave tells them I'm coming.

I shoulder my pack and straw hat and wait. Red stands by me.

"You probably want to leave that bag here, Terra," he says, nodding toward my pack. He holds a large pack with a metal frame and a bedroll out to me.

"Everyone has to carry their share on these trips, and that bag won't do. You'll need a bedroll, food, and clothes."

Nell comes over to stand by us and laughs. "Red doesn't get to go, so he micromanages."

I shrug off my bag and Red hands me the big pack.

"I took the liberty of packing yours. Hope you don't mind. You just need to put your clothes in." He smiles at me. I grin back.

The people here haven't stopped surprising me. They stand in stark contrast to the mob at Town Hall. I bob my head up and down, hoping he'll see my gratitude. He shuffles side to side a moment, rubbing the back of his neck. He searches for something to say.

"Two days ago was hard. But life's not always that way. You can't let it have its way with you."

I carefully pull my clothes from my bag and fold them in the top of the framed pack. I probably should have done this up in my room, I think as my hands close around the first-aid kit in

154

my bag. The sleek metal container is so different from the baskets that hold their own hand-knitted bandages. I glance around, but everyone else tends to their own packs. I try not to look too secretive. I'm trying to be one of them; I am anything but. I slip the first-aid kit into my pack.

I point to my bag and then upstairs.

"Just going to drop it off, eh?" Red says. I nod. "Good. I'll let Dave know and then you'll be off."

When I open the door to Dave's room, I drop the bag on the big bed and turn to go. Hazy rays light dust motes floating through the open window. The long grass beyond the paved road rasps gently in the wind, drifting ahead of dark clouds rolling in. This is so different from the coldness and violence of the city. I'm glad I never told Jessa about this, never asked her to come with me. I hear the sound of my sister's voice, see the tears on her face, hear the heartbreak in her words. I ripped her apart, but she is safe. I glance at the door. No one is in the halls. I lean down to my bag and unzip the pocket that holds the words I've clung to.

I love you too, I think as I press the paper to my chest. I wonder what Jessa is doing. I kiss the letter and carefully fold it. I'm just about to put it back in the pocket when a voice startles me. I whip around.

Mary stands in the doorway. How long has she been standing there? Panic bubbles in my throat as I clutch the paper. It crunches as my fingers tighten around it. Look away, I tell myself. But her eyes catch me and flame at me, not accusingly, but as if she tries to burn a hole straight into my soul. She wants the truth, and I can't give it to her. I can give Mary nothing but lies. No wonder she doesn't trust me.

"You ready?" She shakes off the animal posture she had assumed when I glanced at her. I wrench my gaze from her, and try as casually as I can to put the letter away. My hands shake. Surely she sees it. She is like a dog that senses fear.

I put my bag under one of the desks. I wipe my sweaty palms on my pants. Mary's face is carefully blank, but as we leave the room, her eyes dart to my bag half-hidden in shadows. But there's nothing to be done now.

When we leave the school, Nell hugs me.

"Have fun, Terra. And be careful. Most of these boys will tell you what fun a hunting trip is, but Red would be the one to tell you to be careful. It's often best to listen to my Red." She squeezes his hand.

"Just stick with Jack, you'll be fine," Red says.

But I need Dave. Jack is quiet and thoughtful. Dave laughs and jokes. I need that to keep myself from thinking. I understand now why there was a bonfire—a distraction. Why a hunting trip—another distraction. I understand why we need *so many* distractions.

We pass through the grass next to the oca fields. I glance back one more time. Nell stands in back by the fire pit, waving. I wave back. Nell is so open, she seems to embrace all of us with that farewell gesture. Dave sidles up next to me. He acts like the past two days didn't happen. I love him for it.

"She always waves until we're out of sight. Sometimes I think it kills her to be away from all of us for too long. She's like a mother to us." He turns back to our path. Sweat breaks out on his forehead, the faint, glistening beads reflecting the morning sun.

I think of my pack unguarded in my room. I shudder.

156

"You okay?"

Why am I so stupid? Why did I have to pull that out and read it? This is why I had my tongue carved out of my mouth. But that hadn't mattered after all. Now Mary is suspicious and I still can't say anything.

I jump when Dave puts a hand on mine.

"You sure you're okay?"

I realize I've been wringing my hands. I try to smile, but it comes out like a grimace.

"You've been funny since we came back from the drop. What's going on?"

The drop. The last thing I want to talk about. I try a better smile. I need to change the subject. I point ahead and glance a question at him.

"Where're we going?"

I nod. He adjusts his pack on his shoulders and brushes the hair out of his eyes before putting on a wide-brimmed hat.

"About thirty miles away. West southwest. I couldn't even tell you what the place is called. Or used to be called. Someone before my dad used to call it Olympia or something. But that name kind of disappeared and we just call it the hunting grounds. It's where we always go."

I flinch. Thirty miles? In these hiking boots? I have a few good blisters already from walking through the city, and I've been too embarrassed to ask for any moleskin. They all thought I walked here from Arizona. Blisters should not be a problem.

We pass the first scanner at the edge of the woods. It is waist-high and black.

"In theory it only activates when a tracker is within fifty feet of it," Dave tells me. "You really don't have these in Arizona?"

157

I shake my head.

Dave shrugs. "Then it scans the tracker and sends the data back to the capitol. In theory. But we're always a little wary."

It remains silent as we pass, not even a mechanical whir to let me know it spies on us. Even though none of us have trackers, we collectively hold our breaths until we're all clear.

We walk through forest on nothing more than a sliver of path through the trees ("a deer track," Dave tells me), and my feet find every root and fallen log to catch on. The other guys with us try hard not to laugh. I honestly think they try. But who can blame them for a few chuckles now and then? I am used to tiled hallways and short carpeting. Here I spend more time splayed out on the ground than upright. Dave spends most of his time with me bringing up the rear.

It is gloomy in the forest, too. Not a sad gloomy, but mysterious. With the clouds that rolled in to blanket the sky, there isn't enough sunlight. Under the green canopy, the light is grayish and murky, like the choppy water when I first landed. If Dave weren't walking so close, I might feel nervous. But Dave walks confidently and talks now and then in his usual cheerful voice.

This is all so foreign to me. I thought life here was farming. Then I thought life here was a race for survival through the city. Now life is a hike through the trees. It's all too new and it's wearing me out.

By the end of the evening, my feet are killing me. We walked about eighteen miles. Dave helps me set up my tent. All our tents circle to face the fire that Sam builds. I go in my tent for a moment while Dave sets up his own. I have to take my boots off. I ease them off as I stifle a gasp. My socks show pinkish wet marks. My blisters probably popped and the pus has oozed

158

through my socks. I'm tempted to take my socks off to survey the damage, but decide not to. I don't want to see that mess, and it will probably hurt worse than taking off my boots did. And I still have to get the boots back on my feet.

Tears stream down my face as I lace up the boots. How do these people walk up here with these heavy boots? Everyone has similar shoes. Maybe I just need more time. I can get used to this life, surely. I have to if I'm going to survive. I will myself to forget the pain. I wipe my face with my sleeve and step outside.

Dave waits for me, a small gun in his hands. "This is for you."

I blanch.

"I know, I know. You'd rather not. And after the boat ride, I don't know if you'd ever use it. Keep it in your belt if you want and never take it out, that's fine. I'll just feel better knowing you have it."

I gingerly take the gun and ease it under my belt. The nausea rises in my throat, knowing I have a gun in my possession. Dave smiles.

"It's just metal and gunpowder, Terra. Metal and gunpowder. It's not dangerous unless you let it be."

He's trying to comfort me, but it doesn't work. I turn from him and sit down on a log by the fire. He pats my shoulder with one hand and goes to help with the cook pot.

Jack sits down by me. "How's your first hunting trip?"

I smile and point to the gun at my side.

"Dave already armed you? I figured it wouldn't be long. Do you know how to use it?"

I nod hesitantly. I do know how. But I remember the tremor that shook me the first time I pointed it at a human being. Can I ever do it again?

Someone brings us each a tin mug of hot water. They boil all their water to purify it, and on a hunting trip, they don't have time to wait for it to cool. The weather is still too warm and sticky for hot water, but I'm parched. I slurp it, and my healing tongue curses me.

Jack sips his. "You know, Dave really likes you." He tries to say it casually, but Jack is always serious. His eyes flick over to me, and then back to his mug.

I can't help smiling. I always smile when I think of Dave, and I am thinking of him more and more. I lace my fingers around my mug and nod slightly.

"I'm sort of the doctor for the settlement. My great-grandma was a doctor, too. She taught my grandma once everything blew up. Then she taught my dad. It was rough—there was no real school or great equipment. The skill is valuable. The government says they offer free medical care. But more often than not, people disappear—to labor camps or worse. The government has no money to offer anything for free—I don't know how they do the supply drops—and no one has any money to pay. Some gangs are willing to kill for a good doctor."

I see a boot on a face, a crying girl, Red alone. My mantra of terror. Jack notices. He sits his mug on his knee and regards me for a moment. His dark hazel eyes glitter in the firelight.

"Were things that different in Arizona?"

Where I came from, it was different. I hope he won't produce a paper and pencil for further answers.

"Yes, it probably would be. Desert and all. You're probably worried more about surviving the weather than surviving each other."

I nod. It is the perfect explanation.

"My dad taught me what Grandma had taught him. He taught me while we left the city—not Seattle, I'm from the middle—to find something better. We wandered awhile before we found Dave and his bunch. They were glad for the medical help. We were glad for something different. Gentler."

I came here for something better. Gentler is a good word. In some ways I've found that. In other ways, The Burn is a million times worse. But the things Jack fled from were so much different than what I left. It makes me almost feel guilty to be here. The settlement is a refuge for all these people who fled violence and terror and the nightmares that keep them up at night. It isn't supposed to be a refuge for people like me. What about my life had been so bad? These people would give anything to live in the colony. I study my mug and chug the rest of the water.

I notice Dave across the firelight. His hair shimmers orange in the fire's glow. All around us is dark. Only the people, the tents in fading shadow, and the trees standing so dimly I can barely make out the shapes of their trunks gleam in the firelight. Dave's eyes look gray in the light, and they dance. Dave's eyes are happy, but something veils them slightly. My Dad's eyes have the same veil, but his is so heavy that his eyes are constantly smothered by it.

It is love. That's the difference. I surprise myself at the revelation. My dad had love, but it was gone. Dave had it with Mary. What do other people see in my eyes? Is this why Jessa always begged me to go out with her? Did she see this same shadow in my eyes?

As I look at Dave, I warm from head to toe, and I think maybe the veil is lifting. Dave can protect me. Dave can hold me against the nightmares that come every time I close my eyes. If he kept those arms wrapped around me, I would never be lost again.

Jack gently flicks me with a finger. I jump. He laughs—a gorgeous, quiet laugh. I can't help smiling. I haven't heard him laugh before, and I love the sound. He raises his eyebrows in Dave's direction.

"Yeah, I know who you were looking at." He says it kindly.

I blush and hide my face in my hands. Jack laughs even more quietly this time.

"There's nothing to be embarrassed about. Dave's a great guy. We've been friends ever since I came here."

I grab his hand. He's hesitant at first until he sees I want to spell something on the palm.

"Mary?" he asks. I nod, hoping he'll understand.

"Yes, I could see how that would be a problem. You're smart if you noticed all that already."

He looks up as Sam brings us each a plate of stew with a slice of bread. I take my plate and bow my head to Sam.

"You're welcome, Terra."

And then Jack says, "Sam, what would you tell her about Mary?"

Nothing is a secret here. Everyone will know I like Dave. No wonder Mary doesn't trust me. Sam glances between me and Dave. No secrets.

162

"We all kinda wondered when that would come up." Sam sits on my other side and shovels a mouthful of meat and oca in his mouth. The gravy drips on his smooth chin, and he dabs at it with a rough cloth napkin. Most of the guys here have whiskers. Sam is hard pressed to grow stubble. He's at least a year younger than me. I think of him driving the boat with a gun pointed at his back.

"The thing with Mary is that she and Dave talked about getting married."

I almost choke.

Jack thwacks me on the back. "Well, he's eighteen. She's almost twenty. I don't know how they do it in Arizona, but up here, marriage often happens sooner. It's safer to always be with someone."

Sam takes a sip of water, stabs a shriveled carrot with his fork, and opens his mouth. Then freezes.

I look up. Just outside the firelight between two tree trunks a solid shape materializes. Not tall and straight like the trees, but shorter, stockier, and two gleaming pin pricks shining back at us.

Dave sees it too, and makes a quick motion with his hand.

Sam lowers his voice. "Guns ready." He puts his plate down and stands up slowly.

Dave's eyes never leave the shadow man. He snaps his fingers and Sam and two others flank him. Sam's hand rests casually behind his back on the gun in his belt. I can barely hold a gun. He's younger than I am. He shouldn't have the responsibility of one.

Dave doesn't have a gun. He looks so vulnerable without it.

He clears his throat. "Hey, stranger. You want a meal? Come on into the firelight and have a bite." There's a steely edge to his kind words.

The man takes three slow steps forward, his hands raised submissively. The firelight finally touches his face, and his eyes shine like daggers. His gaunt cheeks are lined so deeply that his face looks scarred. His lips stretch so tightly they are nothing more than a white line in his face. When the man is about ten paces away, he stops. He lowers his hands to his side.

"What's your name, friend?" Dave asks.

My eyes flit to Sam. His hand tenses on his gun. The other men in the circle stand statue still. This is a very dangerous situation, and everyone knows it. Before the supply drop, I might not have understood how dangerous. But now my palms are so slick with sweat, I can barely keep a grip on my gun.

"Smitty." His voice rings with false friendliness. Am I the only one who hears it? The other men sit down, still eyeing the stranger, not completely off their guard.

"Welcome," Dave says. "We always have enough to feed a lone survivor."

"You're nomads?" Smitty asks, shifting his weight, looking at our tents. "No home camp?"

Dave nods his head. "Yup, we're nomads. We mostly roam south of here, decided to try up this way for some more game."

A gleam comes in Smitty's eyes. But Sam must read it as curiosity. His hand falls from his gun.

"Lots of game up here?" Smitty asks.

Dave nods. "Lots of deer, a few bears." He's still stiff. He inclines his head slightly toward Sam. He doesn't like that Sam let down his guard. I am far enough away that Smitty won't see

164

me slowly take my gun out of my belt and turn off the safety. The click is deafening in my ears, but Jack doesn't even flinch.

"Sorry to take any more of yer time. What I really need is a doctor. My wife tripped a few miles from here. Fell and twisted her ankle good. I don't know if it's broken. We were by a city, but I didn't want to take her to the clinic."

Everyone nods their heads. No, no one wants to go to a clinic. Sympathy eases the tension slightly.

"Told her I'd be gone for a few hours to see if anyone was about."

Jack blanches. Why is he so nervous? I lean to him. He looks up at me, fear scraped into his eyes.

Dave relaxes a bit. "Sorry to hear about that, Smitty." He ushers the man into the fire circle. He hands him a plate of food.

"We have someone who knows a bit about medicine. He and a few others could go with you to check on your wife."

Smitty looks up hungrily at all of us, his eyes roving. He tries to pick out the doctor among us and says distractedly, "Not too many. I want to get back to her quick."

Jack quivers next to me and tries to hide in my shadow. What's wrong with him? He looks up at me, pleading. He doesn't dare say anything. And then I remember what he said. *Willing to kill for a good doctor.*

My head snaps up so sharply it hurts. Are there more eyes watching us from the trees? Or are they several miles off to avoid a gunfight that will inevitably bring agents? Smitty still hasn't noticed the two of us back here. How can I tell Dave not to say anything more? Not to let Jack go with only a few men?

That there is a bigger gang lying in wait for them? I feel the certainty of it in my gut. If Jack and the others go, we will never see any of them again.

Dave's eyes narrow. He knows something's up, but he can't focus on it yet. "I'll send enough," he says. "Jack, up here please."

Jack lets out a soft moan only I can hear. He drags himself to standing. I clench his hand but he refuses to drag me along with him. He will walk to his doom alone.

I stand behind him, hoping Smitty won't notice me or my gun as Jack approaches him. Smitty smiles, his white lips curling into a chiseled grin.

"Thank you kindly, friend," Smitty says to Dave, not even looking at him. He can't take his eyes off Jack. "Come with me, Jack is it? My wife is in the woods this way."

He gestures to the trees. Dave raises a hand.

"Wait a minute, stranger," Dave says, finally starting to come close to what must be nagging him. "I said a few would go with."

But Jack is already there, already next to Smitty. He clamps down on Jack's arm with a white-knuckled hand and with the other pulls a long, vicious knife and jabs it against the delicate skin at Jack's throat. He twitches the knife once and a small thread of blood slides down Jack's neck. Jack closes his eyes.

I see the girl crying in the alley, Red all alone across the interstate, Black Hair with a rifle aimed at Sam's back.

Then one thought alone explodes in my brain so strongly that the rest of those scenes fade except for Smitty's vicious face. He could take this life away from me.

He turns to point the knife at Dave. Smitty opens his mouth to speak, but no words come out. Instead his eyes widen in surprise because with a clap of thunder, I blow a hole in his chest.

FOURTEEN

I slump to the ground as Smitty slumps, the gun falling with a scuttle of pine needles. I tremble all over and can't stop the shakes, even when I wrap my arms around my legs and hold them so tightly I ache all over.

Then Dave is there, talking to me, but I can't understand what he says, because I can't hear him. I moan and babble in my tongueless language, and tears course down my cheeks. He strokes my hair back from my face and picks me up in his warm arms and carries me away from the dead body fifteen feet from where I lay. He shushes in my ear and cradles me like a child.

I don't want him to see me, to see the person who could do such a thing. I smash my hands against my face, and all I can smell is the gun shot on my fingers. The cry chokes in my throat, and I throw myself away from him and into the trees.

"Terra! Come back!"

And vaguely I hear someone else say, "Get her right quick. No telling how close the others are."

A quiet part of my brain knows what this means, knows it is a warning, but the rest of my brain tells me to run. This man I love could never love someone like me. A liar. A tongueless freak. A murderer.

As I run, I realize that my feet ache and I can't go any farther without screaming at every footfall. I slow down then, enough that two huge arms grapple me and tackle me to the ground. I struggle, but I'm too exhausted to fight long. I lay limp.

"Terra. Are you okay?"

Why does he ask me so slowly, enunciating every word?

The tears start again. I roll from him and hug my legs and wonder if in a second I will run again. He would chase me. I wonder if we will repeat this for the rest of our lives.

Then he says something so unexpected it knocks all thoughts of running right out of me.

"The first time is always the hardest."

I can look at him, then, if those words mean what I think they do. He nods.

"When I was twelve. Some scout for a gang found my mom in the strawberry fields alone. Thought he was far enough from the school for anyone to see him. He didn't realize I was coming out with some dinner for her. I shot him as soon as I saw him. And when he fell dead, I shot him three more times."

He is close enough in the darkness that I can see his face, and it looks haunted.

"I think about it every day. The scary part is that I'm not sorry."

He eases away from me then, giving me space to let my sobs ease. His face is ghostly in the dimness, but I know he is real, and that reassures me. He stands and offers a hand. I take it. He wraps an arm around me.

"I can't say it'll get better. It doesn't. But you come to terms with it."

I'll have to believe him. He weaves us back through the trees. I step carefully next to him, not sure whether I can trust my aching feet. When my boot hits a rock, my foot explodes with pain, and I slump to the ground again.

"You okay?" Dave asks, suddenly there. I nod. I can't tell him about my feet. It will give me away in a heartbeat.

When we make it back to the fire circle, all that remains of Smitty is a faint depression in the ground where his body fell. Thinking his name makes me nauseated. My gun is nowhere to be seen. Jack stands at the edge of firelight, waiting for us.

Dave doesn't take his arm from me, but Jack hugs me and holds me tight. "Thank you," he whispers. "Thank you for listening."

He doesn't want to let go, so Dave eases me out of his grasp. We walk away toward my tent, and Jack watches us, unable to move.

Dave unzips my tent and helps me sit. "I'll sleep right out here tonight, Terra. I won't be far. I'll just go get my bedroll, okay?"

I nod numbly, not sure if I want anyone around me right now. From the sound of it, we are all murderers. How can we ever live with each other? How do they live with each other every day? The empty pit in my stomach spreads to my chest. Then it will spread to my head. If it reaches that far, what will be left of me?

I left the colony to find a place I belong. Instead I find I am capable of unspeakable violence. Would Jessa even recognize me now?

I shudder and crawl into my bedroll, pulling it up above my head and curling into a ball. If I curl myself up tight enough, maybe I can contain the nothing that seeps into my blood.

Leaves muffle the sound of Dave settling down in his bedroll just outside my tent door. I watch his shadow on the far side of my tent, as he props himself up on one elbow to gaze at the fire. His shadow glances back every few minutes. Is he hoping I'll call to him, or reassure him I'm alright? I can do neither.

I feel like one of the dangler fish bumping into the colony windows. Shining a beautiful light that leads to nothing but ugliness and teeth, and I am completely blind. What am I doing here?

I'm an outsider. A liar. I've begged for their food and shelter and friendship. What have I given them? The only thing one of them said *thank you* to me for, was for killing a man.

I cry again, sobs wrenching out of my chest. I gasp under the weight.

My tent door opens and Dave stands there, uncertain what to do.

"Can I come in?"

I can't see him from under my bedroll, and he probably doesn't know what to do with an unhinged murderous girl.

I can't do anything but let the searing cries work their way out of me. Dave scoops me up, bedroll and all, and holds me.

"Shh," is the only thing he says as he rocks back and forth. He strokes the bedroll where my head is and shushes me until I hiccup with the fading sobs and fall asleep.

I wake up with my eyes crusted shut, and my cheeks ache with dried tears. The gray light of early morning shines through my tent walls. I thought the world had shattered last night, but here it resumes. Faint murmurs surround me, the sound of the other men waking and starting a fire, warming food for breakfast, making the sparse, whispery conversation of early risers. The world is sharp, and I notice everything.

A weight hangs over my shoulders. Dave lies next to me, his arm draped over me and his fingers loose with deep sleep. His brows furrow slightly, and his mouth twitches. A sigh of air escapes his lips. Even in his sleep he shushes me.

I am still here; the nothing didn't swallow me whole last night. And I realize I'm wrong about something. Jack told me thank you for saving his life, but he also thanked me for listening. I listened to him. Has no one else ever done so? I remember the way he begged me with his eyes, how I was the only one he looked at. Has he told no one else of the gangs who murdered for medical treatment? That doesn't seem right. I've been here only a matter of days. Why would he tell me?

I roll my stump around in my mouth. Why did Nell tell me the things she did? And Dave? And Mary of all people? Because I can't speak and they can't hear any judgment from my lips? I tried so desperately to be a friend to them that they surely don't see any judgment in my eyes. Maybe I *am* good for something to these people.

I shrug Dave's arm off and sit up. I pull my knees up. This is new to me. In the colonies, your worth was determined by how well you could perform a task. I had failed five vocations. I felt pretty worthless. But I never realized I have this kind of talent with people. A talent for friendship and trust. That's surely worth something. Especially to people who are hunted, who fled dangers they would rather not speak of.

Dave stirs and stretches his long limbs. His eyes focus and he looks over at me. What he sees must surprise him, because he blinks several times before a smile turns his mouth up.

I smile shyly back at him. With this new clarity about myself, I realize just how much I need him. The thought shocks me. It burns me from my toes to the ends of my hair, and I almost break out trembling with it.

Dave's lips part, but he doesn't speak. I nod to him encouragingly.

"You're okay?"

I nod again.

"You're sure? You were pretty unhinged last night."

I rest a hand on his to reassure him.

"I've seen that happen before—the first time someone has to do that."

I appreciate the way he says it—that it isn't something someone would *want* to do.

"But most people aren't quite as shaken up by it. By the drop, too. Like you've never seen anyone killed before. That's pretty uncommon, you know."

And I want to live here, in this world where it is common to see people killed. I may be a good listener, but I may also be crazy.

"I wish you would tell me all about life in Arizona. It sounds a million times better than up here. It sounds like it could be pleasant."

I shake my head. True where I come from there isn't murder. But it is a prison.

I grab his hand. With the world too clear and focused, I want him to know me. Even the colony. But I drop his hand abruptly. This is what I promised, this is the price: no one will ever really know me. He doesn't see the chill come over me. He brushes a loose strand of hair behind my ears.

"How did you know about Smitty? How were you the only one who saw it coming?"

It takes a few minutes to spell out the story that Jack told me.

"I never knew it was that bad. Poor Jack."

Dave wraps an arm around me and leans his head against mine.

"Well, thank you. For listening to him and watching. And doing what needed to be done. It's not something you ever want to think about again. But thank you."

My heart flutters at the intimate touch, but I don't reach any closer to him. I can't trust myself or my longing.

Dave stands up and unzips the tent.

"Smells like breakfast's almost ready. You want some?"

I expect the hollow place in my stomach to lurch with all this thinking about what happened last night, but it remains quiet. I am ravenous. Dave offers a hand and helps me up. I wince as the pain stabs through my feet.

"You sure you're okay?"

I nod and signal just a moment to him. He leaves.

I dig around in my pack for my first-aid kit. I can't ask for precious painkillers for my feet. But my first-aid kit has some, and I'll need them to get me through this hike. I gulp a couple down and stuff the rest in my pocket.

Breakfast is fried salted fish and hard cookies studded with dried strawberries. I gnaw on a cookie and sip hot water. Jack walks slowly over to me.

"Hey, Terra."

He shifts his weight side-to-side, one hand holding his plate, the other scratching his arm uncertainly. His dark brown hair is ruffled from sleeping.

I glance at the log next to me, and he's grateful for the invitation. He hems for a moment, opening his mouth to speak and then closing it again. Only to open and close several more times. I've never seen him this unable to articulate himself. He's usually so thoughtful with his words. He finally closes his eyes.

"I hope when you look at me, you don't see *him*."

And I know *him* is Smitty. No. I put a hand on his shoul-der. He pats it awkwardly, but I see the relief in his face.

"I really like you, Terra, and I think we could be great friends. I don't want one person's horrible intentions to ruin that forever." As he speaks he holds my hand more firmly. His eyes glitter.

He jumps when Sam is suddenly by us, clearing his throat. "I realize you two are having a heart to heart. But is there room for me?"

Jack grins and makes room. Sam gazes straight into the fire. "I have your gun. Dave says not to give it back unless you want it."

I don't want it. I will never touch another gun for as long as I live.

"I didn't think you would." Sam looks down at his plate and pokes a cookie with his fork. His next words are softer. "I'm sorry about last night. I should have been more careful, should have seen what Smitty was. It should have been me."

I ache for this boy who would have killed in my place.

Dave comes over and sits on my other side. He glances at all of us. "Seems I leave for a minute and I miss everything," he says cheerfully.

Jack laughs again. "That's what you get for leaving her."

"I'll have to work on that."

My heart flutters again. Dave smiles.

"If the weather holds, we'll make it to the hunting grounds tonight. This cloud cover makes the traveling easy and not too hot. As long as it doesn't turn to rain, we'll be quick."

Sam leans in to me. "The trail's a little wider the further we go. More dirt. As long as it doesn't rain, it'll be hard-packed and easy to walk."

Dave whistles, and all heads turn to face him.

"Anyone else still need breakfast?" Everyone shakes their heads. "Then let's get packed up and head out."

I wash out the pots in a stream just beyond a thicker copse of trees. A person-sized pile of rocks lays about twenty feet from the opposite stream bank. I turn from it before I can ponder too closely on what it covers.

The painkillers help my feet, and I refuse to take my shoes off to inspect the damage. I don't want to know. I can't see the sun through the trees, so no one can rightly say what time it is. I hear a helicopter fly overhead. We all pause. I look up, but the cover is too thick. We keep moving.

This leg of the trip is harder than yesterday's. The ground rises, and we rarely go downhill. The terrain is rockier, although

176

even the rocks are hard to see for all the moss and growth. We rest by a small cluster of boulders that have managed to avoid getting blanketed in anything green. Jack tells me we are about five miles from the hunting grounds.

When no one is looking, I take two more painkillers from my pocket and swallow them.

By the time we reach the hunting grounds, I'm practically sleeping on my feet. Dave stands next to me, hand on an elbow, guiding me along, ready to support me if necessary.

He tries to take my tent from me and set it up, but I wave him off. I need someone, I need to be alone. I confuse even myself sometimes. My mind is foggy with too little sleep and things I try not to think about. I need to keep my hands busy.

"Oh, come on, Terra! You're exhausted! Doesn't help that you're emotionally exhausted, too. Let me at least help."

But I shake my head and try to recreate the way he did it the night before. When I finish, I'm proud of it. As I leave it to go eat dinner, I ignore the way Dave scurries around the tent, pounding in the stakes I forgot about.

That night, one of the men brings out a small metal rectangle and blows into it as he slowly slides his cupped hand across the other side. I grip Dave's arm.

"A harmonica," he says. The word is unfamiliar. I definitely haven't learned this one before—I would remember. Nothing prepares me for the wailing, hauntingly beautiful sound. Dave grins. "You've never heard one before?"

I shake my head and watch, transfixed on the sound and the way the man who plays it closes his eyes and leans into the music. Then Sam's sweet voice rises in song.

"Amazing grace, how sweet the sound," he sings. "That saved a wretch like me."

I've never heard it before, and it pierces my heart. Mr. Klein told us about the superstitions on the Burn, what they call religion. He explained how the colonies were founded by scientists and they left all superstition on the surface before coming into the ocean. Mr. Klein called it a great loss.

I don't really understand the meaning of the words—I have no context. But something this lovely and assuring has to be more than just mere superstition. It has meaning beyond just the words and the music, I'm sure. I would willingly spend the rest of my time on the Burn just to figure it out.

Dave leans over. "Terra, are you crying?"

I touch my cheek and realize I am. He gazes at me tenderly. I touch my heart. Dave nods.

"It's a beautiful song, an old song, and nobody sings it like Sam. That song has carried a lot of us through a lot of things."

If Jessa had asked me just a few days ago if a song could have helped me through *anything*, I would have laughed at her. But in a matter of moments, I've changed my mind. The emptiness in my chest eases as I listen.

I lean closer to Dave, the spell of the firelight and music working into my soul. He doesn't pull away. Instead he wraps an arm around me, his hand gently pushing my head onto his shoulder.

"I'm glad you found us," he whispers. Then his lips brush my hair.

He sleeps just outside my tent that night, and I ache for the weight of his arm over my shoulders. But I won't ask for it. I can't make demands because I cannot be completely honest with him. This will be his choice.

Most of the men are gone by the time I wake up, leaving a smoldering fire and just me, Jack, and one other to see to the camp. I miss Dave already.

"We'll clean up breakfast and get things ready for whatever the others kill," Jack says, stacking plates to take to a stream and wash. I gather up the utensils. "We need to find a good place to string them up to drain." He tries to say it all casually. I can tell what happened two nights ago still haunts him almost as much as it haunts me. But he doesn't want to think about it. Doesn't want to talk about. He keeps himself busy. We're alike.

I take his hand. *Drain?*

"Didn't you go hunting where you came from?"

It's different.

He shrugs. "It probably is. We need to let all the blood drain out of the carcasses. Then we'll carve up what we need and carry it back to the settlement."

My stomach lurches as I think about all the blood that will soak the ground. An image of a pile of rocks by a stream flashes through my mind. Jack holds out a hand. He notices how pale I am.

"But don't worry—you don't have to do that part."

I nod gratefully and take the pile of dishes from him. I will be the designated dish washer. I will cook. I will do anything— as long as I don't see more blood.

The day is punctuated every now and again by a gunshot in the distance, but they happen so infrequently that I'm startled every time I hear one. Our other companion fills the cook pot with meat and vegetables to make stew for dinner. He is a largely quiet man who rarely speaks. But we enjoy his friendly silence as he smiles and nods, and he is the hub to our activities around camp.

The camp is a small meadow. A fire pit occupies the center. It is a large fire pit, larger than the one at our camp last night. The stream is close, providing washing and drinking water. And scanners stand guard around the perimeter, placed every twenty feet. I grab Jack's hand and write a question.

"Oh, we found this place quite a few years ago. Dave's dad decided we needed a place to go hunting. He didn't want to rely on the government food drops—you've seen why. He didn't want anywhere near the settlement because he didn't want gunshots giving away where we were. So they scouted around a bit and decided on this place. We come every few months. As you can see, the government also realized we come here." He nods to the scanners. "So far they haven't set up a video feed, so we're okay for now, as long as no one with a tracker comes with us."

I hadn't noticed the scanners last night, but now I feel their eyes on me. They look like headstones in a cemetery.

I barely notice when the gray sky deepens toward evening. I am helping Jack throw some lines of rope over a heavy tree branch just barely within sight of our camp when I notice the dark shadows emerging from the trees and converging on the fire. I tap Jack's foot and point.

"Good, they're back." He clambers down from his perch in the tree and we thread our way back among the trees to where the hunters are returning.

Between them, they carry a small black bear and a deer.

"Not bad," Jack says, smiling. "Terra and I set up some lines in the trees over there. Our usual tree must have fallen since the last time we were here, but those look strong enough."

The hunters take the game to the trees. I watch as the hunters take the rope and deftly tie coils of it around the animals' hind legs. Then they work together and heave the animals up into the trees so their heads dangle down. Sam takes out a long glinting knife and stands before the bear. I'm about to turn away, but I am not quick enough. In one swift motion, he slices the knife across the animal's throat and a gush of blood runs down the bear's head and to the ground. I close my eyes, but I still see it burned red in my eyelids. I stumble back through the trees.

Dave is there by the fire, lifting the lid to the cook pot. He watches me, concern on his face.

"Had enough blood for a while?"

I nod. He scoops himself up a plate of stew. He offers me some, but I shake my head. My stomach roils. I know my appetite will come roaring back with a vengeance and all the dinner will be gone by then, but right now I can't stomach it.

That night we sit around the fire and sing. I hum along as Sam sings that song again. Dave settles close to me. Jack sits protectively on my other side—my unofficial guardian. I couldn't have lost him even if I tried, I think. Not that I mind. Jack is sweet and kind and loyal. But Dave's presence pulls me like a magnet.

Dave senses it too, and he asks Jack to make sure there aren't any other animals too interested in the carcasses. Jack wanders away, and looks over his shoulder once at me. Then he disappears behind the trees.

"Hmm. I think he's come to admire you," Dave says.

Jealous? I write in his palm. He laughs. He pushes his blond hair away from his forehead and glances over at me. The fire flames dance in his eyes. He smiles sheepishly.

"Yeah, a little."

I lean away a fraction and raise my eyebrows.

"Okay, maybe not in an angry, 'I've got to pound his face in,' kind of way. But yeah." He traces the shape of my cheekbone with his fingers. His fingers are rough with calluses and tug slightly at my skin. I shiver under his touch. Then he leans forward, and my breath catches in my throat. Does he hear my heart pounding against my ribs? It is ready to burst out of my chest; it's almost comical to me. But my lips won't smile about the joke—his are too close. His eyes close slightly, covering the flames whirling across the blue. Then his lips brush mine gently, just enough to make my lips burn.

I open my eyes and he's sitting up again, looking back to the fire. How long have I been here with my eyes closed? But no one is even watching. Jack hasn't returned yet and the others still sing and talk softly in the fire glow. Only Sam looks over and winks once. I just smile back.

But Dave says nothing to me for the rest of the night.

FIFTEEN

We stay at the hunting ground for one more day of hunting and a day of getting the meat ready to take back. The others kill another deer and a huge bull elk. Almost everyone is occupied with dressing the meat, but I remain carefully busy taking painkillers on the sly and helping Jack around camp. I glance at Dave now and then, but he doesn't look at me.

The next morning, all the extra cargo is distributed among us. I carry one of the huge skins in my pack—it isn't as heavy as the meat, apparently—but it still weighs me down, and I don't know how much more my poor feet can take.

As we follow the narrow trail back the way we came, I'm right about my feet. All the painkillers do is take the edge off, and I grit my teeth without realizing it. We come out of the feet of the mountains, back to the flatter regions that surround the hunting grounds. I tell myself it should be easier. The trees are still huge, but they aren't huddled so closely together as they were further up. The ground is hard and dry. It should be easier.

Some of the others around me grumble now and again. All of them know the return trip would be harder. Why hadn't I counted on it?

When the crops had fully matured on Field #3, we just used the harvester, then lowered the feed belt to transport the crops through the maze of tubes to land in Food Storage. I really don't even know what path the belt followed or where Food Storage even is. I have never been there. I was supposed to have seen it at one point or another—you see just about everything in the colony so you know about where you live. But I think that was during one of my vocation stints that went south—cooking—and I avoided learning anything more than I had to. All I know is that we ended up eating what we had grown. Someone down there prepared it, though I hadn't personally enjoyed talking to any of the food preps. I wasn't the most social person.

So what? How did I expect a huge hunk of meat to make it from the hunting grounds thirty miles away back to the settlement? We all carried, and we were all weighed down. I can't believe I didn't think of it. I'll get it, though. I'll figure it out.

I hitch up my pack with an awkward and grimace-inducing bounce. The change of balance sends daggers through my feet. The sweat on my back makes my pack slide around. As I carefully tiptoe over a crude log bridge, Jack tells me it will take us an extra day to get back with the weight. That's fine with me, screaming feet and all. It's an extra day to figure out the weirdness that suddenly wedged itself between me and Dave. An extra day to avoid Mary's wary glances.

The thought of Mary brings anxiety slamming full force into my gut. She'd seen me read the letter from Jessa, and she'd seen me put it away. Can I trust the sense of honor that most people

184

in the settlement have? Can I trust her not to search my things? My instincts tell me no. Not Mary who has been scarred so deeply and is so fiercely protective. I should have never left it alone. But it's too late now. A sudden crow call makes me jump. I am stretched so tight I feel like my bones might break through my skin.

The next day the gray sky opens and misty rain floats down in wet veils. I wear a poncho, but I am too warm and sticky inside of it. I finally run out of painkillers, and my wet socks rub against my raw feet. It's all I can do to keep from crying. That night instead of eating dinner with everyone, I retreat to my tent. After dinner, Dave stands outside. He breaks the uneasy silence between us.

"Missed you at dinner, Terra. You okay?"

I make some muffled, gurgling sound that I hope sounds like a yes. But Dave unzips the door and steps in.

"Whatever, you're not okay. You were too hellbent on the trail today, nothing but staring straight at the ground. And then you don't eat dinner. Come on, what's up?"

I've hidden it for too long, and the pain in my feet screeches at me to come clean. Traitor feet. I point to my boots.

"Something wrong with your boots?"

I nod.

He takes one boot and unlaces it, then unlaces the other. I squeeze my eyes closed and my breathing comes in shallow rasps. Even unlacing my boots is agony. He eases them off and I stifle a scream. I must sound like a dying animal. Then Dave takes a quick breath.

"Oh, Terra."

His bleak tone makes me open my eyes. I look at his stricken face and then down to my feet. My socks are worn through in several spots and are bright red with blood.

"How long have your feet been hurting?" he whispers. He's unable to move, to take his right hand from my boot and his left hand from my heel. Now that my boots are off, my feet feel much better. I look at them with detached interest. I've seen so much blood the past few days, surely all this can't be mine.

"Terra? Do your boots not fit right?"

My feet do slide in them. But I assumed that is the way boots are. They look too big on everyone else, with their thick soles and chunky laces. They're nothing like the slippers I wore in the colony. Doesn't everyone have boot problems? But no, they don't. It's just my boots that don't fit right.

"Why didn't you say something?"

Because I'm an idiot that comes from the colonies, I want to tell him. But I shrug. He rolls his eyes at me. Frustration and anger side-step around the edges of his calm.

"I'll have to admit, Terra. That was pretty dumb to go for thirty miles with boots that don't fit."

I nod. Dumb. Exactly how I feel.

"We'll have to peel these off so Jack can treat your feet. I'll go get him."

I slump a little. Why does anyone else have to know about me and how stupid I am for hiking in boots that don't fit? Dave notices the movement.

"You're seriously worried about your pride right now? You should be more worried about being able to make it home."

186

Of course. What would they do for a survivor that can't even walk? I could never allow them to carry me the whole way. I nod him out the door.

When they return, Jack sits down by my feet while Dave settles near my side. Jack opens his pack and pulls out a few knitted bandages and a small jar of brown salve. He glances at my feet now and then.

"So Dave tells me you like to wear boots that are too big."

His conversational tone makes me laugh despite the pain. He has a good bedside manner. He would have made a good doctor in the colony. His thin lips grin impishly at me.

"Okay, Terra. I'm going to peel off your socks. The rain soaking through loosened everything up, otherwise your socks'd probably be crusted to your feet. This will hurt. Just hold Dave's hand or something. Try not to scream. We don't want to scare the whole camp."

I can't tell if he's joking about the scaring the camp thing. Dave offers his hand and I squeeze it. He pats my shoulder.

"Okay, here we go." And Jack peels off my socks.

I don't scream. I'm proud of myself for that. But I can't sit stoically through it. I clench both hands and arch my back. Dave is a rock, though. He sits and lets me crush his hand. I look down at my feet while Jack gently washes them off.

"Not too bad, really. Just a bunch of blisters you didn't take very good care of. I'll put some of this on them." He holds up the jar. "Nell mixes this up for me. Then I'll bandage them. We'll stuff your boots so your feet don't slide around."

"Will she be okay to walk?" Dave asks. I can see the concern for me, but now that he knows I'm okay, the silence creeps back between us. He's more concerned about dealing with me as extra weight when everyone else is already loaded down with meat.

"That's up to Terra." Jack dabs the thick salve on my feet. "It'll really hurt, but it's fine to walk on."

The silence Dave gives burns me, and I nod briskly and turn away.

"You sure you're okay with it?" Dave says. "We can't slow down."

I've come this far, haven't I? And now my feet will be tended to and not slide around in my too-big boots. I can do it—I have to do it.

Dave looks unsure for a moment, but then the leader side of him nods. "Good."

Jack rolls up the leftover bandages and nestles everything neatly back in his pack. "It shouldn't be a full day tomorrow anyway. We made good time today, despite the rain. And the trail eases up a bit once we're out of the trees. No more rocks and roots jutting up."

Jack comes in my tent before everyone's up and gently removes the bandages, his long slender fingers working deftly over my feet. He applies more of the thick goop, and then he wraps my feet in clean bandages and meticulously stuffs my shoes so my feet fit snuggly inside. My feet ache, but the pain doesn't shoot up my legs like it had last night.

Dave leads us out of the last of the trees and into the wide swathes of grass that mark the last few miles until we reach the settlement. Home. Jack offers a hand when I look unsteady.

188

Something has niggled at the back of my mind since I ar-rived. The way Jack hovered near Dave and Mary that first day at the beach. I grab his hand.

How do you fit in all of this?

He looks at me quizzically.

With Dave and Mary?

He nods. "I wondered if you'd ask. Well, Dave's been a good friend for a while. If you haven't noticed, Dave's a good friend to a lot of us."

I have noticed that. After the silence was broken between us after our kiss, I also wonder if he is just that—a good friend. Nothing more. I let my hand down to trace along the wisps of grass growing waist high. Jack watches the the ripples spread out around us.

"He asked me for advice when things first started up with him and Mary. She was different then—softer, if you know what I mean."

He looks overhead. Sunbeams shine in translucent rays through a slit in the clouds. "Kind of a balmy day, isn't it?"

I look at the sky, at the way the sun shines down in ribbons. I strain my eyes to see if I can see the settlement yet. We're still too far off. Jack clears his throat.

"Anyway, I told him he should follow his heart. And he did. They were going to get married."

I nod once.

"But Mary said she needed to go to Seattle first. See if she was needed there more than here. She invited Dave along, but I think he took it wrong. He thought she needed to see if Seattle was more important than he was. Or something like that. I think they were both confused. I don't know why Mary took off the way she did. And then she was gone for so long and things were really different when she got back. I was there for Dave while she was gone, when he was so messed up thinking she wanted Seattle more than she wanted him."

I nod. It made sense, I guess, and I stumbled into the middle of it. To someone like Nell it probably sounds ridiculous. You're either together or you're not. I like Nell's way of thinking better. And if I like that thinking better, where does that leave Dave and me?

As we eat lunch, Dave sits by me, gnawing on a strip of salted meat, not really allowing himself to look at me.

"Your feet alright?" he asks. I nod. He's strangely distracted. I tap his hand, but he ignores it.

"I think we're about three miles from home. We should make it in about an hour or a little more."

Then the dread nags at me. I'll see Mary; Dave will see Mary. That thought makes me either a little grumpy or a little brash. Whichever one, I grab Dave's hand.

Are you excited to see Mary?

His eyes shift to me then.

"Why do you ask that?" He looks confused and slightly angry. But I don't think he's angry with me. I can't read the reasons for any of it. I take in other details—the peeling skin on the center of his bottom lip, the splash of freckles across his nose. His eyes bore into mine. I shrug. I just wanted to see what his response would be.

"Look, I know you've been open with me, Terra."

How can he start any speech like that? The guilt fingers through me. I've been anything but open.

190

"I know you have, and I'm sorry I can't quite return it. Mary and I are . . . complicated. I'm trying to sort it out. Really I am. But it's not easy for me."

I don't want some fuzzy middle ground. I want all or nothing. So I do something completely stupid and I grab his face with both my hands and pull his lips to mine.

He kisses me back hard, like he's testing something out, finding an answer. The kiss is empty. He pulls back only when Jack walks up beside us.

"You, um, almost ready to move out?" Jack says with a chuckle. But the laugh leaves me cold. He doesn't approve of this.

Dave rubs his hands on his knees and stands up. "Yes."

Jack stares long at me. I watch them walk away, and the burning in my heart tells me it won't be the last time I'll watch Dave walk away. It unsettles me, but I can't do anything about it. We are either together or we aren't. I keep reminding myself all the way to the settlement.

When the school comes into sight, Dave straggles back to me. We walk past the fields blooming with white flowers. They look magical in the hazy sunlight, but I can't bring myself to admire them.

"A wonderful sight, isn't it?" A broad smile spreads across his whiskery face.

Then I look up and my heart freezes. Mary waits for us at the back of the school. I'm approaching the executioner. She stands with her arms folded, her rifle slung on her back. Her dark hair is pulled back in a tight braid, and her hostile posture screams at me. It softens when she greets Dave, and he gives her a warm hug, but as soon as he passes her, the mask is back again. She lowers her voice.

"When you get a moment, Terra, I need to talk to you. In my room, if you don't mind."

I nod. The unsettled feeling returns, stronger than before, and the dread mounts with each tender footstep.

Even Nell's sweet greeting can't erase the weight in my gut. My eyes dart nervously to find Mary. But she talks to Jack, or Dave, or Red, or any of the returned hunters with a belying ease about her that does nothing but mock me.

After our kills are hung in the smoke houses and the fragrant smoke rises in tendrils through the cracks, we all go through the school and close the drapes. I pull thick, itchy drapes over a window, and the beam of light that slashes across my skin dies.

We gather in the cafeteria and eat. We celebrate our return. They weren't as worried as when we were gone for the supply drop, but any separation puts a dim light on the group. No one likes to be the one left behind.

I mechanically put the fork of oca greens and fish in my mouth, hardly tasting it. Jack sits by me and I don't turn to him. It's not until he says, "Terra!" in the voice of someone who's been trying to get my attention for a while that I finally look at him.

I can't focus on his face. I look past him to where Mary sits by Dave, and Dave looks at me. My heart hammers, but the look on his face disappoints me. It is all cheerful friendship. I wonder if any of our kisses over the past days meant anything. Tears burn in my eyes. But I blink them quickly away. I hope Jack doesn't notice.

192

"Mary's going to talk to you?" Jack asks. I start.

"I heard her tell you she needed to. We can both guess what it's about." He nods his head at Dave. Jack puts a spoonful of strawberries in his mouth. They're very dark and slightly mushy. There won't be very many meals with strawberries left.

If only Jack knew. I can almost guarantee that Mary wants to talk about something of much greater significance for all of us. I push my plate away, and it scrapes against the table.

"Are you feeling okay? You didn't eat very much."

I shake my head but offer no more explanation. My stomach roils. I try to will my legs to walk calmly as I leave the cafeteria. Jack watches me go, and I know concern is all over his face. I go up the stairs. I pause outside Dave's room.

I have to know for sure. I have to know if my life here is over. I open the door. My pack is still stashed underneath a desk. I bend down and open the pocket where I left that priceless piece of paper. Jessa's letter is gone.

SIXTEEN

When I go down the hall, Mary's door is already open and she waits for me. I've never been in her room before. It is small. It contains a mattress, one desk, and nothing else. There are no books, no nicknacks, no odd trinkets pilfered from the houses nearby, only a few items of clothing folded neatly and tucked into the desk, with her rifle laid on top of it, and a candle on a plate.

Is this a reflection of her life? Barren? I feel an unexpected wave of pity for her. The set of her mouth makes me quickly forget it. The shiny streaks down her face tell me she has been crying, but now she is angry.

"Looks like I'll do all the talking," she says. Even though I'm expecting it, her baleful tone makes me wince. She reaches to her back pocket and pulls out a piece of paper covered in plastic, folded three times. She has no idea how important that piece of paper is to me. I almost sob just to see her treating it so casually.

"I see you know what this is." She waves it in front of my face. "Hmm. Jessa. A best friend? Or a sister, perhaps?" She seethes with fury, but she isn't interested in my distress. "Whoever she is, it's obvious—you're not from around here, or Arizona, or anywhere, are you?"

I can't lie now. My own weakness in printing that letter traps me. I have to own up to it. I shake my head.

"And then there's this interesting tidbit. I didn't notice it the first time I read through this. I might have passed this off as some message you were able to print off a stolen computer. Until I read the footer."

I groan. I'd forgotten all messages were printed with a footer.

```
Mariana Colony transmission. Do not read
without consent.
```

"A colonist?" Her voice is deadly serious. "We often wondered about colonists. Whether it was just a bedtime story our parents told us. Something the government never wanted us to know. Can you imagine? People living in peace and prosperity at the bottom of the ocean while we scrounge around up here like rats. While we're captured and tortured and killed by our own government. There wouldn't be a single person loyal to the government if everyone knew it for sure. How could anyone *decent* keep that from us?"

I want to explain, to say, "It's not like that, not really. I came here because I hated it down there. Down there isn't real. *This* is what's real." But it sounds so ridiculous even to me. I don't know if any of the survivors here would stay if given the chance to go down. My tongue forces my silence, and she takes advantage.

"Do you have any idea how Dave feels about colonists?"

The idea shocks me. I never dared lean toward any conversation of the sort. I wanted to keep that topic as far away as possible. I shake my head, numb.

"He *hates* colonists."

I hear every implication in that sentence. She should have just said, "He hates you."

"How could you do this to him?" She starts crying again, and the tears course down her face and fall to the floor. "How could you do this to any of us? So many of them trust you. He trusted you. He even let himself like you."

I slump down onto the desk. My body feels so heavy with every lie I told.

She circles around to the doorway, blocking my exit. She is a dark silhouette against the dim light of the hall.

"Of course I won't tell him if you don't want me to." And she holds the letter out to me.

What is she saying? She has to tell him. Isn't that her whole point? Tell him what I am so he'll loathe me and then she will comfort him.

"You heard me right. I won't tell him. If you do something for me."

I know I won't like what comes next. But her cunning surprises me.

"I'm going to tell him I rescued him. And you're not going to say otherwise."

My hand slips off the desk then, and I have to catch myself so I don't collapse on the floor.

She folds her arms. "You see the significance of that. I knew you would. I also know you were there that day. That was when you first came here, wasn't it?"

I nod blankly, not even looking at her anymore. Not looking at anything, just feeling the empty spot in my stomach start to expand and punch holes in all my vital organs.

"I know you were the one who pulled him out of the ocean. But he doesn't know that. And you can never tell him because then you'd have to change your whole story. I know the way he's mooned over this mysterious rescuer ever since it happened. Dreaming he's in love with her after only a moment. Love doesn't happen that way. But if he believed it was me, then maybe things can go back to the way they were. The way they were before I left."

I wonder if she really does love him, or just loves the idea of him. If he is the only thing that kept her alive in Seattle. The thought of him. Was that why she finally came back? He was the only good in her life?

And again I feel that strange pity welling up in the last remaining full spot in my body. I am a tin man—hollow. Except for my heart. My heart is full to bursting, and it bursts out through my eyes as the sobs I fought to contain suddenly wrench themselves free.

She watches me cry and her face is a kaleidoscope of emotion. Even though she has destroyed me, she takes no pleasure in it. She merely wants to protect Dave and the colony. Then she hands me a paper and pencil.

"Any last words?"

I nod and write three words. The only words I have for her at that moment. I could write so many things, I could lash out in anger and frustration, could beg her not to go through with it. Instead I write:

I am sorry.

Then I hear a sound at the door and I turn. Dave stands there. Confusion is all over his face. Seeing him stand there is more than I can bear. I run from them.

"Terra?" he says as my footsteps echo down the hall.

"Just let her go," Mary says.

I slip downstairs and out the double doors before anyone can see me or stop me. I'm not sure where I'm going, but away is the best I can do. I follow the same paved road I had followed when I first came here. I trudge along, my feet aching. Past the sad houses and the water treatment plant. Past the marshy areas. I am slow. I am tired and hungry and emotionally drained. I am torn between two homes, and I can have neither.

The sky is well dark by the time I reach the beach with its rundown parking lot and debris-covered sand. The old boat Dave almost drowned with has washed ashore and is overturned, half buried in the sand. I sit on it, not even minding the damp that soaks through my pants. I gaze out to the water and watch it ripple in the moonlight. A faint blue light flickers at me from the water. I didn't know the moon could shine in colors. But then I look closer and realize the light moves beneath the water. Then it surfaces.

The sleek gleam of a sub rises above the water. I jump up. Someone has come for me. Would my father actually break all the laws of the colonies to come here and fetch me? My heart rises a moment as I hope that he might. That he loves me more than he loves the colony.

The sub slowly inches forward, then sloshes into the sand and stops. The hatch opens. A teenage girl with a buzzed head appears from the dark hole.

"Jessa?" I try to say. Seeing her made me forget for just a moment that I can't speak. I can't believe it. I've thought of her countless times the past few days. She's beautiful.

"Terra? Oh Terra, I've missed you so much."

She flings herself off the sub and into the surf and runs to me, tripping in the sand she isn't used to walking on. Then she is hugging me tighter than anyone ever has. She cries into my hair and squeezes me. I cry with her and kiss her cheeks. But where is her hair?

"I had no idea if you were dead or what happened, or if I would ever find you. I couldn't tell if Gaea was laughing at me, or lying to me, or what."

I pull back, shocked. Jessa nods, wiping the tears from her cheeks.

"After a week went by, I just about went crazy. I missed you so much, and I didn't know if you were dead. Mr. Klein noticed how weird I was acting in class. He called me to his office one day and gave me a note telling me how to find her. Told me she'd have answers. So I went."

She is brave. I never thought she'd find Gaea and come here. I hug her again.

"Gaea told me where you'd gone." Jessa looks at me closely. "She also told me what you paid."

My empty mouth aches with every word I can't say to her.

"I don't completely understand why you did it, but I under-stand enough. I paid too." She runs a hand over her scalp. She gave her hair to Gaea. Her great beauty, her one vanity. She gave it up for me.

She's more than her hair. She's more than her hair. I tell myself over and over. I do it to keep from crying again as I look at her stubbled head. She shakes her head, waking herself up from her thoughts.

"Look, I don't have much time. That sub is programmed to turn itself around. I came here for a reason. I want you to come home."

I drop her hands then. She wants me to go back to the colony?

"I asked Gaea how I could get you back. She must be watching you or something. She knows that someone named Mary knows that you're from the colonies."

I frown. What does this have to do with my coming back?

Jessa pulls a small metal cylinder from her pocket. "Don't open it yet."

I take it from her. I turn it over a few times in my hands. It's lightweight and fits easily in my palm.

"A hypodermic needle's in there. Filled with poison. Enough to kill a person. She understands that it needs to be subtle so no one else would know what you did."

I step away from her. Nausea rises in my throat. What is Gaea asking me to do? What is *Jessa* asking me to do?

"Look, don't freak out, Terra. Gaea said as long as Mary's left up here without you, she could talk. But if she dies in her sleep, then no one knows any better and you can come home."

She must see the horror on my face.

"I know it's horrible, Terra, but it's the only way. Please? For me?"

200

I shake my head, shaking the fuzz loose that gathered as soon as she said "kill a person."

"I know it's a lot, Terra. Just think about it, okay?"

How can I even think about it? I've seen too much death.

"She's our mother, you know." Jessa says it impersonally, like we're talking about an insect. "Gaea, I mean."

As soon as she says it, I know. I didn't realize it then, but I know. It explains the spite toward my father and the loving hatred of the colony. The knowledge doesn't move me. I feel no tie to her. She mutilated and silenced me. She took Jessa's great beauty. No mother should do that. No mother should ask her daughter to commit murder. She and I have both become monsters.

The sub engines begin to purr again. Jessa turns around.

"No! Oh, Terra the sub's going to go back. I need to get on it. Look, Gaea's sending a sub to come tomorrow night—midnight. Please get on it. Please. It'll only stay for fifteen minutes and then it'll go back to the colony. Please, Terra."

And she skips toward me to kiss my cheek one last time before running to the sub, clambering up to the hatch, closing it behind her, and then she is gone. The only evidence she was here are her tears in my hair, the tingle of her kiss on my cheek, and the metal cylinder in my pocket.

As I limp back toward the school, I pull the metal cylinder from my pocket and turn it over in my hands. The gravel scrapes under my boots. I don't think about walking or the school or Jessa. My brain is sluggish. The only clear thought I have is *How can I?*

201

After what happened with Smitty on the hunting trip, the last thing I need is more blood on my hands. Did Gaea—I refuse to think of her as mother—watch that as well? Did she sit hunched over her keyboards, her eyes fixed on the monitors as she watched my life unravel? Is the metal cylinder in my hand a sick joke or a gift?

The sour taste in the back of my mouth gags me. Clouds skirt over the moon, and the path in front of me darkens. I stick to the pavement, the only sure way I know of getting back in the dim light. Soon the sad houses line the road. I look long at them. Broken windows, shutters, leaning porches, all of it surrounded by tall grass.

People had lived here, and people had died here. People had been happy here. Why can't I be one of them? I could leave it all behind. I could go back to the colony where I'm not a murderer. Where everyone has enough to eat and everyone lives peaceably, and the brutality up here is just a rumor.

By the time I see the dark school, I hear a voice calling my name.

"Terra! Are you out here?"

I stop. Dave stands outside, his hands cupped to his mouth.

Dave wants me home. Red comes down the steps behind him. Should I go to them? What can Dave offer me? What can he offer me now that the mystery of his rescuer will be revealed, and all I can do is look on? The settlement will never be home again.

But I put one foot in front of the other and walk forward into a pool of light cast by one of the open doors. He sees me.

"Terra! Where'd you go?"

He grabs both my shoulders and looks into my face. I must look haunted. He frowns.

"You're okay?"

I can't move. My feet ache, my head hurts, and I'm falling apart as he stands there holding me together. He won't be able to hold me together much longer.

"Where were you?"

I point behind me. He looks past me, disbelief on his face.

"I would have thought with the way your feet are you wouldn't be up for a walk. But whatever. You're back now." He gives me a hug.

I stiffen. I breathe the scent of sweat and smoke, strawberries and worn cloth. I won't get another embrace like this, I'm sure. I soften and cling to him for only a moment—the only moment I will allow myself. The dull ache in my chest catches at my ragged heartbeat. I close my eyes and etch him into my memory. Then I pull back.

"Come on, let's go in." He drapes an arm over my shoulder.

Why does he make this so difficult? Why does he put an arm around me like I am one of them? I shrug his arm off. I can't let him do this.

I can go home to the colony. I see a girl crying in the shadows. A face ground into the gravel. A man with a hole in his chest. I can go back to the ocean and let the water wash away these nightmares forever.

Mary waits for us inside. I can't look at her.

"Oh, you found her." She surprises me by sounding genuinely glad. As much as I am a traitor and a threat, she doesn't hate me. She worries about all of us. I am too tired.

"Dave, can I talk to you for a moment?"

My knees buckle. This is it. He will be gone forever. The metal cylinder is icy through the thin fabric of my pocket.

"Sure." He looks back at me, worried. He must see how pale I am, how hollow my eyes are. But Mary pulls him around and leads him out again, out to the back where a small fire burns and several of the men are busy tending the smoke houses.

I walk to the cafeteria, now dark, and pull the drapes back just a sliver from a window. Mary pulls Dave a little aways from the others, just out of earshot. But I can still see their faces in the fire glow. Dave, with whiskery cheeks and impatient mouth, Mary with surprising softness in her eyes. She really is in love with him.

They sit down on two folding chairs, side by side, the chairs just barely toward each other. Mary stares at him, but Dave looks at the fire. Then her mouth starts moving rapidly. His eyebrows shoot up.

Part of me wishes to be out there. Covered by the tree just behind their chairs, I could hear their words and see if Dave believes her. I sag against the window. The stronger part of me knows I don't want to hear any of it. Seeing is bad enough.

Dave's brow furrows in deep lines. He thinks hard through what Mary tells him. The disbelief wavers on his face—he wants to believe her. When I see that hope, I know I've seen enough. I know what the outcome will be. This almost home of mine is crumbling.

I leave the window. I go out the cafeteria and up the stairs. Jack waits for me outside Dave's room.

"I wanted to change your bandages before bed."

He shrugs his supply pack off his back. I wave him off. I need to be alone. I have so much to think about I feel like my brain will explode. He sees it on my face.

"It can wait," he says, putting the pack back on. "You know, when I need to be alone, there's a place I go to. Want me to show you?"

His face is open and smooth and kind. I nod.

"Over here." He opens a door marked "Janitorial Closet" and ushers me inside. At the back behind a metal shelf is a ladder.

"This goes up to the roof. I like to sit up there and think sometimes. I feel like I can get up away from everyone, get up above all the stuff that goes on down here."

I put a hand on his, a small thank you. He leads the way up, opening the roof access door.

There is a flat spot up here on the roof, big enough for the two of us. An ancient cooling unit stands guard on one side, long rusted and broken. Jack leans against it.

"I do need to change those bandages before you sleep tonight. When I'm done, if you don't mind, I'll just sit on this side and you won't even know I'm here. I've been wanting to come up here ever since we got back."

I'm about to protest the intrusion. But I realize the silent companionship would be nice. To not feel completely isolated in this world I created for myself.

And then the tears come. I'm surprised how I don't even care that Jack is here. He changes my bandages without a word, working quickly, methodically, and tenderly around my abused feet. Then he leans back against the metal. He keeps his word—

he is quiet and unobtrusive and just stares at the moon that glimpses down at us in occasional cloud breaks.

I cry myself to sleep, curling down on the hard roof top. The last thing I remember is Jack draping a blanket on me so softly I think I must be dreaming.

SEVENTEEN

I wake to gray morning light. The west is still dark, and to the east the water of the sound looks like a rumpled metal sheet. Jack lies under a blanket alongside the big box of rusted metal. His lips twitch in his sleep.

I pull the metal cylinder from my pocket. I open it quietly, glancing once at Jack to make sure he still sleeps. The small syringe shines inside its cocoon. It is filled with pale yellow liquid. A plastic cap covers the needle. The needle would slide so easily into her flesh. It wouldn't be hard at all. I close the cylinder with a faint click.

A rush of hope comes over me. I could go home. I could escape the terror we all live with here. No more waking nightmares, no more blood.

Without waking Jack, I climb down the ladder. My legs and back are stiff from sleeping on the hard surface, but my feet are surprisingly good. I still twinge when I walk, but I don't limp.

At the door to the janitor's closet, I pause. The hall is empty. The settlement still sleeps. I take a deep breath. Then I clench my fingers around the cylinder, the skin of my palm digging into the seam where it opens and closes.

Now. There will be no other chance.

As I walk down the hall, my boots thud so loudly in the early morning hush, I'm sure someone will open a door and wonder what I'm doing. I pause outside Dave's door, my fingers hovering over the handle. I don't want to face what I'll see. I close my eyes. I promise myself no more nightmares. I turn the handle without a sound.

I barely make out the human shapes in the darkness. Dave and Mary sit at the top of the mattress, leaning against the wall. They must have fallen asleep talking. His arm drapes around her shoulder, and her head nestles into the hollow between his shoulder and chest. Her arm rests across his stomach.

I almost choke as I look at them. The love is as palpable here as the warmth of their sleeping bodies. They just needed some miracle to get past their own complications. I provided that for them.

But I promised myself no more nightmares. As long as Mary lives, I will never be at home anywhere.

I kneel down next to the bed. Mary lies one foot from me. I watch her chest rise and fall. A strand of hair falls across her face and her slow breath weaves the hair with the light from the open door.

I open the cylinder. The syringe gleams. My hand trembles as I lift it from the case. It is feather-light, lighter than the gun I used to kill Smitty. It could be a toy next to that weapon.

I pull the plastic cap off the needle. Mary sighs and sinks deeper against Dave. Even in unconsciousness he pulls her closer. They are in love. They always have been. Love is like the ocean. I blink that I can compare something like love to the ocean I grew to despise. But it is. It is like the ocean I could see outside the sub window as I came here. I could see for only a few hundred feet, but it reaches for miles.

Watching them I realize I'm not in love with Dave. All I thought about was what he could give me. I haven't given him anything. He gave me home and family. I gave him lies. As I watch them sleep, I understand the truth.

The needle is a lethal inch-long dagger. Only eight inches to close the gap, raise the sleeve of Mary's shirt, and I can return to the colony. But I know my promise of no more nightmares is empty. This will be one nightmare I will never wake from if I kill Mary as she sleeps in Dave's arms.

His eyelids flutter and his lips purse slightly. I can't do this to him—can't do this to them—now that they've found each other again.

I hear footsteps in the hall. I quickly sheathe the needle and jam it into the cylinder and back into my pocket. As I slip through the door, I chance one last look back at them. They belong together.

In the cafeteria, everyone gathers for breakfast. Nell sits by herself, waiting for Red. I sit with her. She smiles at me, but I see the worry in her eyes. I'm not sure why until I notice Dave and Mary two tables over. Mary leans her head in close to his and Dave has his arm slung about her.

I look back at Nell and try to smile. She pats my hand and doesn't ask any questions. I'm grateful. She think I'm broken hearted, and I am. Just not for the reason she assumes. I will never see Jessa again, and I couldn't even tell her I love her last night.

I sip my tea. Nell leans over to explain she has been experimenting with herbal teas to give some flavor to the boiled water. She frowns when she tells me she hasn't created any really good blends yet. These are the details I will miss. Then Red joins us.

"But it's still better than hot water," he says. He too looks over at Dave and Mary. It seems everyone in the cafeteria glances their way periodically. Mary surprises me by not meeting any glances, not soaking in the surprise from everyone. She is only interested in Dave.

"Mary's sure, well, different this morning." Red puts his fork in his mouth. Nell looks quickly at me, but I carefully arrange my face to look uninterested. She squints. She isn't convinced.

"Yes, dear. Love will do that to someone." She kisses him. He turns to put a rough hand on her cheek.

"Powerful thing, ain't it?" Red says. He smiles at her and turns back to his breakfast. They don't say anything more.

I realize I don't belong here anymore, not where I can't even be a friend to Dave without an ache in my chest, not where Nell and Red are so in love that their love colors the world. I'm not ready for that, I don't trust it yet, not for myself. I still need to come to terms with the terror of the Burn.

I can't stay here. I need to carve out my own life and not wedge myself into everyone else's. I realize that now. If I'm to be happy on the Burn, I need to make it mine and not just insinuate myself on it. I need to stop grasping at straws.

Maybe that was my problem all along in the colony as well. I tried to fit where they put me. But I never put myself anywhere. I was never proactive. But I can change. I have a choice.

After breakfast I go upstairs. I make sure Dave isn't in his room. Just as well. I grab my pack. I'm out the front doors before anyone stops me.

"Terra?"

The one voice that could make me hesitate calls out to me. I try to keep going, but he calls me again, urgently this time.

"Terra, please."

I stop. I can't cause him anguish. I turn and see the pained look on his face and my heart aches. Too many goodbyes. He can see the look in my eyes, the pack on my back, the way I walked out the door without looking back.

"You're leaving?" He brushes the blond hair from his forehead. It stands up wildly.

I nod. His eyes dart around, searching for something.

"I don't understand."

I reach out to him, touch his arm. I need to tell him I'll be okay. This is the only way I'll be okay. His fingers graze mine. Even that small touch sends shivers up my arm. I have to turn around before I change my mind.

"Why?"

I raise an eyebrow. Surely he knows why. Is everything so black and white to him? We are friends, I should stay, even though he's in love with Mary. That's just the way his honest heart sees the world.

I couldn't be happy, I spell out on his hand. He holds my hand a fraction of a second too long.

Why is he doing this? The tears start in my eyes again, and they put him out of focus, turning his edges softer, softening his lips and his smile. They make him look unreal. Maybe this is the way I saw him from the beginning, when I should have just seen him as he is—a confused teenager, like me.

"You weren't the one who rescued me that day." He wipes a tear from my cheek. "But you did save me, you know. I'll always love you for it."

I ease myself free then. This isn't helping me leave. I just look at him one last time and turn south past the oca fields.

I'm not sure where I'm going, just away. I half expect to hear helicopters beating through the sky, but the morning calm envelopes me and clears my head. After I've walked for an hour or so, I come to the sound. It glints gray at me, chopping in the wind. The wind blows my hair into my face and stings my eyes. I stare at the water.

The Burn is exactly how my dad told me it would be. Vicious, violent, full of blood. I will always have those nightmares. But there are things he couldn't have foreseen. Things no one could guess at. The healing love that spreads here among good people; the friendships; the acceptance. These are things I never found in the colony. These are the things engraved in my heart.

I had lived in the water all my life. Now for some of the most terrifying, blissful, heart-rending weeks, I've lived on the land. I feel more alive than ever before.

I reach into my pocket and pull out the metal cylinder. I walk ankle deep into the cold water. It bites at my toes. I reach back and hurl the poison as far as I can. I see a faint splash where it hits the water. I am lighter now without that burden on me. I feel as if I could ride this wind. The world opens up before me.

I take a sip from my canteen and continue southwest, away from the water and the city across the sound. Then a voice calls out.

"Hey, wait up!"

I look behind me and Jack jogs toward me, his pack heavy on his back, a canteen strapped to his belt. His cheeks flush and the wind blows his brown hair into a halo. I didn't anticipate this.

"I'll go with you, you know."

I shake my head. He can't. I grab his hand roughly.

They need you more than I do. Who will be their doctor? Who will take care of them?

"They managed without me before I came. They can manage now. I've already talked to them about it."

He grabs his pack straps and looks at the ground where our feet disappear in the grass.

"I'm not like them, Terra. The supply drops, the hunting, the guns—I just can't do it."

I know what he means. It's almost a relief to be away from it. He grabs my hand. Not tenderly, but familiarly. We're alike.

"I'll go with you. I may not be what you're looking for right now, but you'll need a friend. I'll come with you."

And those magical words bring the first true smile to my lips in several days.

We turn and walk through the long grass together.

Terra's story continues in *Infraction*

Violent nomads. The coming winter. Jack's unspoken feelings. Leaving the relative peace of the settlement is more difficult than Terra ever imagined. But what she should fear most is the government that professes to protect its citizens. Imprisoned in a labor camp, Terra learns just how much the corrupt regime wants absolute control. Never has she felt more powerless to act. But there's always the call of the ocean, and her captors just might underestimate how powerful that call can be.

Check out annieoldham.com to find out more.

Away from her writing, Annie is the mother of the awesomest girls in the world, has the best husband in the world, and lives in one of the prettiest places in the world (the Wasatch mountains are breathtaking!). She loves to cook, sing, pretend she's artistic, play the piano, and participate in community theater.

Made in United States
Troutdale, OR
03/12/2025

29705307R00126